U0923454

Zadie Smith

扎迪·史密斯作品

使馆楼

[英] 扎迪·史密斯 著　黄昱宁 译

上海译文出版社

目录

使馆楼

0－1

谁能料到会有什么柬埔寨大使馆？没有人。过去不会有人想得到，现在也不会有。在我们大家眼里，这就是个意外。柬埔寨大使馆！

大使馆隔壁有一家健身中心。另一侧是一排私宅，多半都是富庶的阿拉伯人（反正我们这些住在威尔斯登的人都是这么说的）。他们的大门两边通常会竖着科林斯柱，后院还有——反正大家都相信有——游泳池。

相形之下，使馆楼也显不出什么气派。那只不过是一栋位于伦敦北部郊区的别墅，四五个卧室，建于一九三〇年代，四周围着八英尺高的红砖墙。在这堵墙顶上，不时有一只羽毛球飞来飞去。他们在柬埔寨大使馆里打羽毛球。击球，扣杀①。击球，扣杀。

惟一能说明大使馆果真是大使馆的，是大门上的一块小铜牌(上面写着："柬埔寨大使馆")，还有飘扬在红瓦屋顶上的柬埔寨国旗(我们猜想那是他们的国旗——难道还会是别的不成?)有人说，"哦，不过好歹这房子四面有高墙，这就说明它跟街上其他房子不一样，不是私宅，而是一座大使馆。"说这话的人可真蠢。明明很多私宅也围着高墙，跟柬埔寨大使馆一样高——可它们不是大使馆。

---

① 原文是"pock，smash"，pock 是摹拟击球声响的象声词。

0－2

8 月 6 日，法图第一次经过大使馆，当时她正走在去游泳池的路上。那泳池很大，尽管跟奥运会不能比。如果要游上一英里，你得打四十一个来回，过程无比单调，对精神的考验常常不比对体力少。水总是异常温暖，好取悦大多数光顾健身中心的客人，他们并不怎么热衷游泳，宁可懒洋洋地靠在池边，要不就是来蒸个桑拿，让身体放松放松。法图在这里游过五六回，通常她都是整个泳池里年纪最小的一个，别人都年长她好几十岁。这里的顾客一般都是白人，要不就是南亚人或者中东人，不过如今法图间或也能在水中找到几个非洲同乡。这些大个子男人像小娃娃那样瞎扑腾，费尽力气就是为了不让自己沉下去，她看在眼里，想起几年前在阿克拉[①]加勒比海滩靠自己揣摩就学会了游泳，不禁得意起来。她不是在酒店泳池里学会的——酒店雇员是不许进泳池的。不，她是在度假村墙外的那片风高浪急的灰色大海上挣扎着学会的。浮起来，沉下去，浮起来，沉下去，四周泛着脏兮兮的泡沫。没什么游客踏上过这片海滩（到处都是

---

① 阿克拉(Accra)，加纳首都。

垃圾），至于跳进那冰冷的、变化莫测的海水，这样的人就更少了。酒店里的其他女佣也都没来过。只有几个莽撞的十几岁男孩会在半夜里溜过来，而法图是在清晨。在加勒比海滩游泳和在健身中心里游泳几乎没法相提并论，健身中心里的水温是那么惬意，水面平静得像是在浴缸里。在去泳池的路上，法图经过柬埔寨大使馆，看见一只羽毛球在高墙顶上飞来飞去，看不见打球的人。那羽毛球沿着一道长长的弧线缓缓向右侧飘过去，劈头遭到一记重扣往回落，这情形周而复始，前一个打球的人总是有办法瓦解对方的扣杀，然后再一次把球打出舒缓而飘逸的弧线。更高处，太阳努力想从那灰色的、积满水分的云层中钻出来。击球，扣杀。击球，扣杀。

Sains

0－3

几年前，柬埔寨大使馆第一次出现在我们这一带时，有人说，“呃，假如我们是诗人，看到大使馆突然出现在这里，没准能写出一首颂诗之类的玩意。”（因为大使馆通常都在市中心。我们这是头一回在郊区看到使馆楼。）可我们终究也不是什么诗兴盎然的人。我们是威尔斯登人。我们的趣味总是乏善可陈。打个比方，我怀疑，我们这些人，但凡是头一回从柬埔寨大使馆门前经过，无论男女，人人都会立马联想到那个词儿：“种族灭绝”。

0 - 4

击球，扣杀。击球，扣杀。今年夏天我们看了奥运会，越来越习惯于运动员的嘟嘟囔囔，以及人们发出的其他那些跟奋力拼搏、意志胜利扯得上关系的声响。可是，那两个在柬埔寨大使馆的花园里打球的人却静默无声。（我们也拿不准那是不是花园——墙那边的景象我们看不到多少。那也可能是一块砌着砖的地盘，专门用来打羽毛球的。）惟一表明里面确实在打羽毛球的，是羽毛球在动，挑高，扣杀，挑高，扣杀，轮番进行，而且总是在法图去健身中心游泳途经此地时发生（每周一上午刚过十点）。必须说明的是，在健身俱乐部里有会籍的并非法图本人，而是法图的雇主；他们一点儿都不知道她会这样用他们的会员入场券。（德拉瓦尔先生、德拉瓦尔太太，还有他们的三个孩子——十七岁，十五岁，十岁——跟大使馆在同一条街上，这条马路足有一英里长，大使馆在一头，德拉瓦尔家在另一头。）只有每周一德拉瓦尔先生开车去埃尔特姆照看他开在那里的便利店，而德拉瓦尔太太到他们家开在肯瑟尔莱斯[①]的第二家便利店管

---

① 埃尔特姆和肯瑟尔莱斯都在伦敦近郊。

账时，法图的冒名顶替才可能奏效。在德拉瓦尔一家常住的宅院里，有一张仿路易十六时期的螺形托脚小桌，在它狭长的抽屉里能找到一堆入场券。除了法图，似乎没人记得那里还搁着这些券。

8月6日(她第一次注意到羽毛球)之后，法图每回去游泳之前，会故意在使馆楼对面的公交车站上停留五到十分钟。对她而言，这一小段无所事事的时光几乎是她无力负担的(德拉瓦尔太太到午饭时间就会回来)，可她似乎对此也无力抵挡。使馆楼就是有那么一种诡异的摄人魂魄的气息。通常，经过一番等待与观察，法图一无所获，不过有几次她看见有人抵达大使馆，然后看着他们被传唤进门。尽是些背着帆布包的年轻的白人。他们往往看起来邋邋遢遢，哪怕天气凉意袭人，也照样穿着凉鞋。至今还没发现哪个访客一眼能看出是柬埔寨人。这些年轻人可能是来办签证的。他们听到蜂鸣器传唤就穿过大门进去，可是法图看不清让他们进去的到底是什么人，除非她能站到公交车站顶上。她能肯定的只有一件事：这些零星拜访对于羽毛球毫无影响，它仍然在按部就班地运动着，前一下轻柔，后一下迅疾，前一下轻而高，后一下重而低。

Métroline
98
WILLESDEN
98

0－5

8月20日，奥运会选手们已各自回国许久，法图发觉那花园的远角冒出一个篮球架，白色化纤绳结的篮网高出墙顶，能看得见。但是没人打篮球——至少法图路过时没人打。又过了一星期，篮架朝靠近法图这一边的墙移了一点(肯定是个活动篮架，底下有脚轮。)法图等了一星期，两星期，但篮球还是没有代替羽毛球，后者一如既往。

0－6

当我说柬埔寨大使馆的出现让我们大吃一惊时，我并不想暗示使馆楼的外形有什么奇特的地方。说实话，这条又长又宽的马路上有好几栋怪模怪样的建筑，相比之下，柬埔寨大使馆实在显不出一丁点奇特来。有一栋宅子名叫“加里兰德”，这个词下面还用阿拉伯文刻了点别的话，无论是英文还是阿拉伯文，都镶嵌在几根粉绿相间的大理石柱上，后者支撑着一面巨大的围墙，比使馆楼的墙高出一大截，更适合充当军事堡垒。车辆进进出出时，那扇戏剧性十足的金色大门会自动开启。无论何时，“加里兰德”的车道上总是停着少则五辆、多则七辆车。

有一栋房子，门口有一头硕大的粉红色大象，显然是用马赛克瓷砖做成的。

有一座天主教修女院，门前停着孤零零一辆红色的福特福克斯轿车。有一家锡克教的机构。有一栋仿都铎王朝时代的宅子，里面有泳池，十五年前的那个夏天，米奇·鲁尼[1]在西区表演时曾经租下这房子住

① 米奇·鲁尼(Mickey Rooney，1920—2014)，美国著名影视及戏剧演员，从默片时代起一直活跃到二十一世纪初，是历史上演艺生涯跨度最大的演员之一。

过一季。这房子对面是一家昏暗的养老院，有时候能看到几个面貌悲苦的人，身上只穿着晨袍，站在小小的阳台上，盯着栗子树发呆。

所以，在威尔斯登和布朗德斯伯里这一带，我们并不是没见识过古怪的建筑。即便如此，柬埔寨大使馆还是让我们有点惊讶。只不过，这种惊讶多少有点异样。

0－7

德拉瓦尔家厨房的地板上扔着一张《地铁报》，法图饶有兴味地在报上读到一篇报道，关于一个住在伦敦富人家里的苏丹“奴隶”。这不是法图头一回疑惑自己算不算“奴隶”，不过这篇报道虽然简短，却让她确信她还算不上。不管怎么说，把她从科特迪瓦带到加纳的人不是什么绑架犯，而是她的亲生父亲，而且一到阿克拉，他们俩都在同一家酒店里找到了工作。两年之后，她满十八岁，又是她父亲安排她千辛万苦地取道利比亚，去往意大利——前后打点花掉的那笔钱，对他而言可不是个小数目。更何况，法图能念英文——还会说一点儿意大利语——而报上的那个姑娘，除了自己部落的土话，别的什么都不能读也不会讲。没人殴打法图，尽管德拉瓦尔太太扇过她两次耳光，两个大孩子跟她说话的时候也毫无尊重可言，不管她做什么他们都没有一丝谢意。（有时候她听见自己的名字成了他们口中的骂人话。“你就跟法图一样黑。”或者“你就跟法图一样笨。”）话说回来，也有跟报上那姑娘的境遇差不多的地方。自从她来到德拉瓦尔家，就再也没见过自己的护照，而且德拉瓦尔家从一开始就告诉她，她的工资得先扣下来，支付她居住期间吃吃喝喝、使用暖气外加她那个卧室的房租。不过，最后能一锤定音的是：法图毕竟没有被关在房子里出不来。德拉瓦尔家给了她一张公交卡，派她出去买点吃的或者干点别的也不会疑神疑鬼，他们会给她现金，叮嘱她不管买什么，都要把找零和收据带回来。虽说她晚上不出门，可那只是因为她没钱逛街，在伦敦也没什么熟人。而报上那女孩，主人根本就不许她出门半步，从来不许——她是个囚徒。

比方说，礼拜天早上，法图通常会离开那宅子，到 98 路公交车站上跟教友安德鲁·奥孔库沃碰头，一起到吉尔本恩公路边上的耶稣圣心教堂做礼拜。然后安德鲁会把她带到一家突尼斯人开的咖啡馆，一起喝咖啡吃蛋糕。安德鲁在城里当夜班警卫，付账的总是他。每周一法图去游泳。水格外温热，她在半明半昧中满怀感激——不晓得为什么，健身俱乐部总是喜欢让顾客待在如此昏暗的光线中，弄得像夜总会或者午夜弥撒那样。昏暗的光线能帮着掩饰她的泳装实际上只是一件结实的黑色胸罩加上一条普普通通的黑色棉布灯笼短裤。不，总而言之，她觉得自己不能算是个奴隶。

0-8

那个从柬埔寨大使馆里出来的女人看起来既不是特别像“新人”，也不太像“旧人”——既非显而易见的城里人，也不是一望即知的乡下人——很久以前，这种区别在柬埔寨就开始出现了。不过法图对这些词儿也无所谓，她只是因为第一次在柬埔寨大使馆周围看到一个可能是柬埔寨人的家伙，所以颇为好奇罢了。她对那女人既严谨又实用的穿戴风格特别感兴趣——一件灰衬衫紧紧地束进一条棕色宽松裤，一件蓝色防水外套，一顶松松垮垮的防雨帽——就好像她是一个男人，或者是一个跟男人毫无二致的女人。她留着一头乌黑笔直的短发，手上一大把“森宝利”购物袋里装满了东西，这一点让法图觉得有些诡异：她打算把这堆逛街的战利品拎到哪里去？同样让她吃惊的是，原来这个从柬埔寨大使馆出来的女人也在威尔斯登的“森宝利”里买东西，跟法图替德拉瓦尔家采购的是同一家店。她本来以为东方人只去自己的商店买东西，就是那种神秘兮兮的房子。（她相信犹太人也这样。）对这种自给自足的作风，她既钦佩，又多少有点厌恶，不过有一点毫无疑问：这是一个民族保持巨大凝聚力的秘诀。比方说，中国人当初到法图的村子来接管矿山时，当地一直流传着这样的不解之谜：他们吃的是什么，在哪里吃的？他们当然没到超市去买吃的，也没到主路一带的黎巴嫩商贩那里采购。他们自有安排。（不管是在老家，还是在这里，在法图看来，一个民族能生存下去的关键就是——你得自有安排。）

可是，法图又看了一眼柬埔寨女人拎的大包小包，开始疑心这些购物袋是不是很早以前用过的——设计难道一直没变过吗？她越看越相信这些袋子里装的不是食品，而是衣服或者别的什么东西，每个袋子的轮廓都显得太圆、太光滑了一点。没准她只是装满垃圾扔出去而已。法图站在公交车站上，看着柬埔寨女人走到街角，然后，穿过街道，往左拐上主路。与此同时，大使馆里还是有人在打羽毛球，只是这回打得稍有点费劲，因为此时正好吹来一阵方向莫测的风。有一小会儿法图觉得下一个挑高球会被风吹到南边去，球会越过墙轻轻落在她手上。然而，对面那男人发挥得实在是稳定，简直带着十足的邪气（法图很早就认定打球的两个人都是男的），接住了那个正打着飘的球，再打回去——又是一个致命的、直线下压的扣杀。

WILLESDEN · JUNCTIO
Controlled
ZONE
HOTEL
7
DUNNING

DE - DIVINE

0 - 9

法图对那个从柬埔寨大使馆里出来的女人很感兴趣，她这种狭隘的、基本上局限在本地眼界的兴趣肯定会遭人诟病，不过我们这些威尔斯登人倒对她的态度有那么一点同情。说实话，如果我们对这世上每个小国家的历史都了如指掌——不管是他们激动人心的时刻还是安安静静的时刻——那我们哪还有空过自己的日子，完成自己必须承担的任务，更不用说偶尔放纵自己找点乐子了，比如游泳。当然啦，在我们关注的事物周围画一个圈，然后一直待在这圈里活动，这样的想法当然是讲得出一些道理的。可是，这个圈到底该画多大呢？

0－10

法图看见柬埔寨女人之后的那个星期天，她跟安德鲁坐在突尼斯咖啡馆里吃着两根硕大的手指形甜甜圈，里面塞满了奶油和蛋奶沙司，表面上还洒着巧克力糖霜。就在此时，她决定找个合适的说法，向安德鲁提出这个问题。她特地跟安德鲁提起了纳粹对犹太人的大屠杀，因为在整个伦敦，只有安德鲁能跟她聊这么深刻的话题，部分原因是他很有耐心，又对她颇为同情，此外，他毕竟受过教育，业余还在伦敦西北学院里念商业学位。凭着学生证，他有二十四小时免费上网的权利。

“可是死在卢旺达的人更多，”法图争辩道，“这事儿没人提！没人！”

“没错，我想是这样，”安德鲁一边承认，一边往自己那杯咖啡里加了四块糖。“我得去查一查，不过，没错，人是几百万几百万地死啊。他们隐瞒了真实数据，但你可以在网上看到。总是有很多事给瞒下来的，向来如此。好比尼日利亚的官僚政府——他们最擅长数字学，擅长隐瞒数据，为了达到他们的目的而随意篡改。我想了个名头：我管这叫‘恶魔学’。不是‘数字学’——是‘恶魔学’。”

“没错，不过我想说的是，”法图担心话题会像往常那样滑到尼日利亚政府的腐败上去，赶紧推了一把。“我们生来就是受苦的吗？有时候我觉得，我们生来就比其他所有人更容易受苦。”

安德鲁把他那副学究气十足的眼镜往上推了一下。“可是，法图，你忘了最重要的一点。谁为耶稣哭得最多？他母亲。谁为你哭得最多？你父亲。一旦条分缕析，事情就会显得顺理成章。犹太人为犹太人哭。俄国人为俄国人哭。我们为非洲哭，因为我们都是非洲人，不过，即便如此，抱歉，法图，”——安德鲁胖胖的圆脸皱成一团微笑——“如果尼日利亚跟科特迪瓦比赛，我们把你们打得落花流水，那我会笑啊，伙计！我可没法说谎。我要庆祝的。跳啊！跳啊！”

他的上半身扭动起来跳了一小会儿舞，法图不禁——这可不是头一回——想象他如果当个丈夫会是什么模样，可她只能把自己想象成一名妻子，而安德鲁是她十几岁的儿子，很机灵，也肯帮忙，千真万确，可怎么想也只是个儿子——尽管他其实比她年长三岁。她觉得他的婴儿肥和小胡子都很招人烦，这想法肯定是错的。这明明是个好男人！她知道他喜欢她，知道他为人正派，愿意将此生奉献给基督。尽管如此，她身体里总有一部分，沾染着邪气的那一部分，在抗拒他。

“闭嘴。”她说，努力让自己的口气更像是玩笑而非嫌恶，他总算停下了左摇右晃，把双手搁在桌上，于是她松了口气，看到他的表情突然间变得格外庄重。

“相信我，这是自然法则，法图，单纯而简洁。只有上帝才会为我们大家哭泣，因为我们都是他的孩子。这一点非常，非常有道理。你只要想一小会儿就能想通。”

法图叹口气，拿起勺子舀起一点咖啡沫塞进嘴里。“可我还是觉得我们受的苦更多。中国人从来没当过奴隶。他们总是给保护得好好的，用不着承受最糟糕的事儿。”

安德鲁脱下眼镜，用衬衫衣角擦了擦。法图看得出，他准备给她长长见识。

“法图，请你好好想想：广岛的事儿怎么说?”

这名字法图以前听说过，可是有时候安德鲁的高级知识会让她紧张。她总是忍不住要拼命回忆那些哪怕她相信自己以前就知道的事情。

“巨浪……”她开了个头，口气犹疑不定——这答案是错的。他大笑，朝她摇摇头。“不对，伙计！是巨弹！世上最大的炸弹，当然是美国人造的。他们一秒钟之内就杀了五百万人。你能想象吗？你以为，就因为你的眼睛长成这样——他一边说一边用力拉扯两边太阳穴周围的皮肤——“你就总能给保护起来吗？再想想吧。那个炸弹呀，就算你当时没给炸飞，过一个礼拜那玩意也会熔化掉你的皮肤，从骨头上掉下来。”①

法图意识到她以前听过这故事，要不就是换了一

---

① 从这一段的描述可知，虽然安德鲁在法图眼里是“高级知识”的权威，但他把“广岛”与“中国人”混为一谈，公式化的吊梢眼就是他对东方人的笼统印象。

种说法。可是她每次听到这些发生在好久好久以前的苦难，都会隐约觉得有点儿不耐烦，这次也不例外。对于好久以前的苦难，现在还能做点什么呢？“好吧，”她说，“也许人人都挨过苦受过难，可我还是得说——”

“这里有一个可以拿来对照的观点，”安德鲁一边说，一边伸出手抓住她的肩膀。“我来认真地问问你，法图，好好想想这一点。很抱歉我把你的话打断了，可这个问题我想过好多，现在想一股脑儿传授给你，因为我知道你是那种会认真思考的人，跟这些人——”他挥起一只手，指向坐在其他桌边吃蛋糕的人。“你跟我认识的其他姑娘都不一样，她们满脑子都想着什么夜总会，还有她们的头发。你是一个会思考的人。我以前就跟你说过，无论你想知道什么，尽管问我——我会去查，我会调查研究。我可以上网。然后我就把结果告诉你。”

“你是我很好的朋友，安德鲁，这个我知道。”

“听着，我们的友谊是相互的。在这个世界上，你总是需要朋友的。可是，法图，听我的问题。跟你刚才说的话正好相反。上帝有什么必要特地挑选我们来受苦？要知道，比起别人来，我们对他的颂扬是最热烈的。非洲大陆是基督教信仰增长最快的地方！只要稍稍想一想！这根本说不通嘛！”

“可挑选我们的不是上帝，”法图平静地说，视线越过安德鲁的肩头望着抽打在窗子上的雨水。“是恶魔。”

0－11

安德鲁和法图坐在突尼斯咖啡馆里，想等外面雨停，可雨一直下到午后三点还不停，法图说她只能冲出去淋雨了。她可以跟安德鲁共撑一把伞走到轻轨站，任凭他拉着她贴近他那黏乎乎的、体味浓重的身躯。安德鲁要去布朗德斯伯里站赶火车，他们只能在那里道别。有好几次他都试图把伞硬塞给她，可是法图知道，从阿克顿中央站到安德鲁住的那个小单间，还得走上很长一段路，她不想让他为了她而受苦。

“真是个女强人。不肯让别人保护你。”

“雨可吓不倒我。”

法图从口袋里拿出一顶泳帽，那是她刚刚在健身俱乐部更衣室地板上捡的。她把辫子盘成一个发髻，用力拽起泳帽罩住整个脑袋。

“这想法真有创意，”安德鲁边说边笑，“你应该把这主意卖出去！能赚到你第一个一百万呢！”

“一路平安。”法图说，无欲无求地在他脸颊上亲了一下。

安德鲁也亲了她，却毫无必要地多蹭了一会儿。

0 - 12

法图到德拉瓦尔家时，只有头发是干的，但她不等换好衣服就冲进厨房把羊羔肉从冰箱里拿出来，但这已经没什么意义——到晚饭前的这点时间是不可能充分解冻了——然后她上楼从四个卧室各自的柳条筐里把脏衣服拿走。主卧室、法伊祖尔的卧室和朱莉的卧室里都没有人。楼下有一台电视机在发出刺耳的声响。她走进阿斯玛的卧室，没听见什么动静，以为也是空的，就直奔放在角落里的洗衣筐。她刚打开盖子，就感觉到有一只手在用力拍打她的背。她转过身。

最小的孩子阿斯玛站在她面前，嘴张开，像一条鳟鱼。法图还没来得及搞懂怎么回事，阿斯玛就猛地把她手上的那一大堆衣服全拍落下来。法图蹲下去捡。她刚跪到地上，袭击又来了，这回是一脚踢到她胳膊上。她把衣服扔在原地，站起来，被自己的怒火吓了一跳。然而，当她细看阿斯玛时，发觉这女孩正发疯般地对着自己的喉咙打手势，还双手合十做祈祷状，然后又一次指向自己的喉咙。她的眼珠子往外凸。她突然转向右侧，猛地扑到椅背上。当她回头转向法图时，脸色灰白，法图终于明白了，向她跑过去，将她拦腰抱住往上拔，这一招是她从酒店里学来的。

一颗弹珠——玻璃彩球，中央的那抹蓝色像一道海浪——从孩子嘴里飞出来，湿漉漉的，落在地毯的长毛绒上。阿斯玛哭起来，疯狂地大口大口喘息。

法图一面抱住她，一面担心什么时候才能把衣服收拾好。她们一起下楼来到休息室，家里其他人都在那里，从壁挂式平板电视上看“英国达人秀”。看到阿斯玛哭得厉害，大家都站了起来。德拉瓦尔先生按了天空卫视接收器的暂停键。法图把弹珠的事儿解释了一通。

“不要把东西往嘴里塞，这话我跟你说过多少回？”德拉瓦尔先生问道，德拉瓦尔太太用他们自己国家的语言说了一句什么——法图听到她提起他们的上帝的名字——然后把阿斯玛拉起来，让她坐在沙发上，伸手抚摸她女儿那一头顺滑的黑发。

“我喘不过气来，老天！我根本没法叫人，”阿斯玛哭道，“我差点死掉！”

“你到底干吗要把弹珠塞进嘴里啊，你白痴吗？”法伊祖尔说，随即把天空卫视接收器的暂停键松开。“什么样的人会把弹珠往嘴里塞啊？白痴。我打赌你肯定吓得屁滚尿流。”

“哦，她救了你的命。”老大朱莉说，这几个孩子里头法图最不喜欢她。

“法图救了你的命。这事儿可够深奥的。”

“如果换了我肯定会这么做，”法伊祖尔一边说，一边夸张地在自己瘦削的身体上表演海姆立克急救法[①]。“如果这不管用，我就对着自己来两下空手道，嘭嘭嘭嘭嘭——”

“法伊祖尔！”德拉瓦尔先生大喝一声，僵硬地转过身面向法图，其实并不是对着她说，而是冲着她手肘和她脑后那面旭日镜之间的某个点说话。

“谢谢你，法图。还好你在这里。”

法图点点头，走开，可是走到休息室门口时，德拉瓦尔太太问她羊羔肉有没有解冻，法图只好承认她刚拿出来不久。德拉瓦尔太太用自己的语言狠狠地说了句什么。法图等着下文，但是德拉瓦尔先生只是尴

① 即在哽噎者的上腹部迅速向上施压以将异物压出气管的手法。

尬地冲着她笑笑，点头示意她可以走了。法图上楼继续收脏衣服。

0 - 13

“留你无益。除你无妨。”这是红色高棉的一句格言。

这话是在说“新人”，那些不肯抛下城市生活去农场干活的城市居民。政权把人们统统赶回土地，希望藉此创造一个“旧人”社会——也就是说，这个社会的成员都是清一色的农民。新人离开城市，被安置到农村，最要紧是不能在田间地头流露出丝毫软弱来。弱不禁风只会招来死神的惩罚。

在威尔斯登，我们几乎都是新人，只有少数人——好比法图——在不久前还是旧人，在各自祖国的土地上务农。我说的是威尔斯登的旧人和新人；我代表他们说话，尽管他们并没有选过我，而且一定会纳闷我哪来的权力。我可以说，“因为我生在威尔斯登、吉尔本恩以及女王公园的交叉路口。”可是马上会有人骂骂咧咧地回答我：“哦，别犯傻了，好多人都生在那里呢，说这个压根没什么意义。你我不属于同一个民族，谁也没法代表我们说话。这一大堆纯属胡言乱语。我们看你穿着晨袍，站在阳台上俯视柬埔寨大使馆，盯着栗子树，一脸蠢相。你这么说，其实只是因为想不出更好的事情可做。”

0－14

周一，法图去游泳。路上她停下来看了会羽毛球。她想，那只把球往下扣的胳膊，肯定跟她在泳池中笨拙却管用的自由泳动作异曲同工。她走进健身中心，把入场券递给柜台后面的姑娘。在光线昏暗的更衣室里，她换上了那套结实耐穿的黑色内衣。她一边游一边回想加勒比海滩。想起她父亲给平台上的客人端上一盘盘笛鲷，他的蝶形领结总是有点儿歪，想起那些丑陋的游客，整个景象都浮现在眼前。当然，如果在那里看见俊俏的本地小妞坐上德国白人老头的大腿，根本无须大惊小怪，可她永远没法忘记那两个英国白人老太太——其实皮肤发红，拜阳光所赐——两个人都长得肥大，尺寸相当于把两个普通女人捆起来。科威库和奥赛躺在她们俩身边，这两个男孩的胳膊瘦骨嶙峋，搭在女人肥硕的、发红的肩膀上，陪着她们在酒店“舞厅”里跳舞。她们管他们叫迈克尔和大卫，他们诺诺应声，入夜便跟着女人钻进她们的房间，不见了踪影。她认识那两个男孩真正的女朋友，她们跟法图一样，都是客房女佣。有时候，科威库和奥赛前脚和英国女人过夜，后脚她们就得进去打扫。而且她们自己在那群客人里也有“男朋友”。那是个酒店嘛，又不是什么圣洁的地方。而且那泳池呈芸豆形：谁也别想在里面好好游泳，也没人流露出一丁点想游泳的意思。大体上，他们只是站在里面喝点鸡尾酒。有时候他们干脆叫人把汉堡包送到池子里来。法图很不喜欢看到她父亲蹲下身子，将汉堡包递给某个水深及腰的男人。

加勒比海滩上只有一件好事：每月一次，某个周日，会有辆车停在大门口，本地教堂的教友穿着盛装，纷纷从车上拥出来，在庭院中排好队，鱼贯走进泳池，集体受洗。从来没人事先提醒游客，法图也一直不明白这些教友是怎么会获准这么干的。可她喜欢看他们的白衬衫鼓起来，铺展在水面上，喜欢听他们哭泣，听他们歌唱。那一刻——尽管法图并不是那个教堂，也不是任何教堂的信众，那个能让她归属的教堂只存在于她心中——可她还是觉得自己也接受了洗礼，由此便可安全无虞。不知怎么的，她觉得自己之所以跟加勒比海度假村的其他姑娘不一样，正是拜洗礼所赐。将近两年时光——身边既有父亲在耗神费力，也有一个隐匿不见、秘而不宣的上帝的恩典——她在两者之间好好工作，每周日早上天一破晓就去游泳，一切顺风顺水。然而魔鬼却在等着她。

还差一个月就要离开阿克拉的时候，某天早上，法图走进一间卧室打扫，听见门在她背后轻轻关上，她根本来不及伸出一只手拉住。他来了，这一回，是穿着一副俄罗斯人的皮囊。事后，他哭着求法图谁也不要告诉：他老婆去看海角城堡，明早他们就要离开。法图听着他哭得抽抽搭搭，这才明白过来，原来他以为酒店会因为他的行径而责罚他，要不就会报警。就在那一刻，法图恍然大悟，魔鬼非但邪恶，而且愚蠢。她把口水吐在他脸上，转身离开。一想到那个魔鬼，她怒气冲冲，游得飞快，有那么一会儿，她轻易就甩了隔壁泳道的白人小伙子一大圈，其实在他那条泳道上本应游得更快才对。

0－15

“别把你的怒火喂给魔鬼，那是他的美食。”安德鲁告诉她，那是一年前，他们俩初次相遇。当时她坐在吉尔本恩公园的长凳上正吃着一块三明治，他递过来一份宣传散页。“别让魔鬼太轻松。”他不请自来，径直在她身边坐下，开始解说散页上的文字。这散页给印得像一张报纸，他从标题开始讲起：“为什么会有痛苦?”她喜欢安德鲁。他们聊起了神学。后来就这样聊进了突尼斯咖啡馆，每个礼拜天，一直持续了好几个月。他说的好多话她以前都听别人说过，但她从来没被他们说动过，让一切发生实质性变化的是他说的一句话。在此之前，她刚给他讲了个故事：

"有一天，在酒店里，我听见海滩上吵吵闹闹。当时可是大清早。我出门，看见九个孩子的尸体给冲到了海滩上。十岁，十一岁，男孩，女孩。他们先前跳进水里，却不会游泳。有人在哭，也许两个人吧。其余的人只是摇摇头，按着原来的方向接着往前走。过了好久警察才来。尸体给运走了。人们说，'好吧，现在他们跟上帝在一起了。'大伙儿都去忙自己的事，跟之前一模一样。我也回去干活。第二年我去了罗马。我看到一个约莫十五岁的男孩骑着自行车被撞倒。他死了。街上的人都在尖叫哭泣。人人都在哭。他们跟他可不是一家子。他们只是陌生人。第二天，这事上了报纸。”

安德鲁答道，“龙头一旦打开，水流必然飞快。”

0 - 16

又游了二十圈。法图竭力回想她第一次哭是什么时候。在罗马，但不是为了那个骑自行车的男孩。当时她正在一家天主教女校里打扫厕所。那会儿她还不知道耶稣，所以这究竟是哪种学校在她看来也没什么差别——她只晓得要打扫厕所。正午，她有十五分钟的休息时间。她会跑到马路对面那个有围墙的小花园里吸一根烟。有一天，她坐在喷泉附近的一张长凳上，看见灌木丛里有点蹊跷。一罐绿漆。一只金色的喷雾罐。一套装扮自由女神的服装。一张身份证，写着拉杰卜·德万基的名字。一只鞋。一只空钱包。一只塑料桶，顶上有一条狭长的缝，用来收硬币和欧元纸币——桶里是空的。桶上有几点看起来像是血的污渍。在此之前，她一直挺嫉妒民族街上的孟加拉男孩。她觉得她也能把自己漆成绿色，静静地站上一小时。可是每当她想多了解点情况时，那些孟加拉人都不肯跟她讲。这一行壁垒森严，只有棕种人才能介入。她只能待在厕所隔间里。她还以为他们赚那点钱有多容易呢。然后她就看见灌木丛里这一小堆凄凄惨惨的物件，忍不住哭起来；到底是为她自己哭还是为拉杰卜哭，她也弄不清。

最后两圈她换了个仰泳姿势，胳膊放松下来，像青蛙那样向外蹬腿。浸在水中，她想到了更多的水。“只要去我们教堂受洗，所有的罪便能一笔勾销，你就能重新出发了。”安德鲁是这么许诺的。她从来没对安德鲁坦白过自己的罪孽，可她知道他知道她不是处女。2011 年 2 月 6 日，她终于成了一名天主教徒，安德鲁领着头发还没干的法图来到突尼斯咖啡馆，问她感觉怎样。

她兴高采烈！她说，“我觉得自己成了新人！”

可这样的快乐很难持续。次日，法图回去工作，她在离柳条筐还有好几英寸的地板上捡起朱莉的脏内衣时，只能拼命提醒自己，她现在已经跟耶稣建立了新的关系，而这种关系将会改变一切。难道一切并没有因此而改变吗？接下来那个礼拜天，她字斟句酌，向安德鲁表达了这层疑虑。

“可是你难道以为自己再也不会伤心了吗？再也不会生气、疲倦或者干脆就是给人惹得翻了毛腔？——不好意思，我用词不雅。行了，法图！聪明点儿，伙计！

难道想要快乐也是错？

0－17

法图兀自沉浸在这些如水般流动的思绪中，到家比平时稍晚一点，刚进门没几分钟，德拉瓦尔太太就到了。

“阿斯玛好吗?”法图问道。昨天晚上她听到那女孩儿哭过。

“老天，那只是一颗小弹珠罢了。”德拉瓦尔太太说，法图这才意识到，现在的情形完全出乎她想象：

自从周日晚上起，德拉瓦尔家的大人就没法直视她的双眼。“干吗人人都要大惊小怪啊。我给你列了一张清单——在桌上。”

SMALL & BEAUTIFUL

Brondesbu

0－18

突尼斯咖啡馆里，法图看着安德鲁手里端着搁了两杯摩卡和几块可颂面包的托盘，从桌子与桌子之间的空隙中费力地挤过来。他的后背撞在一个男人的手肘上，身上的皮风衣又长又笨，腰带拖到了另一个男人的午餐上，他只好一路走一路向别人道歉。你可没法说他是个举止优雅的男人。但他出手大方，行事周到。她站起身，把一块摇摇欲坠的可颂放回盘子中间。他们同时坐下来，相视一笑。

“你问过我柬埔寨的事儿，”安德鲁说，“呃，这事儿挺有意思。”他敲敲眼镜框。“假如你居然敢戴上一副眼镜，知道会怎样？他们会杀了你。戴眼镜说明你想得太多了。他们的想法简单粗糙。他们想让大家都回到乡下，像普通人那样过日子。”

“可是有时候，在乡下过日子确实更简单啊。”

“在某些方面是这样。我其实也不清楚。我从来没在乡下生活过。”

我其实也不清楚。听到他这么说倒是不错！这是个好兆头。她放肆地朝他微笑。“乡下人的罪孽没那么深重。”她说，可他似乎并没有看出她在跟他调情，只管开始另一场演说。

“那没错。可是你不能逼着别人住到乡下去。我管这个叫‘强人政策’。我在论文里自己杜撰了这个说法。反正尼日利亚那套强人政策的底细，我们都很清楚。他们自上而下地压迫你。总有人想出头当‘强人’的，把什么都收到他们自己手里，告诉所有人该怎么想、该怎么做。其实他才是最脆弱的那一个。然而，如果强人看出你看出他们的脆弱，他们就别无选择，只能杀掉你。这才是真正的悲剧。”

法图叹了口气。“我从来没有遇上什么人不想告诉别人该怎么想，该怎么做。”她说。

安德鲁笑起来。“法图，你把我也算在里面？你现在也是女权主义者啦？”

法图把马克杯端到唇边，用锐利的目光凝视着安德鲁。男人的弱点有好有坏，她已经渐渐认定，事情的关键在于，你得弄清楚你面对的是他的哪种弱点。

“安德鲁,”她一边说，一边把她的手放在他的手上，“你想跟我一起游泳吗?”

0 – 19

法图相信德拉瓦尔家关照过邻居窥伺她的一举一动，所以她不肯让安德鲁周一早上到那宅子来接她，而是像往常那样掐在十点之前出门，手里提着一个给她打掩护的森宝利购物袋，朝健身中心走。隔着很远她一眼就看到了他——这条路是那么直，他到得又是那么早。他站在绵绵细雨中瑟瑟发抖。她颇感歉意，却也有点得意：就是因为想看到她的身体，安德鲁这个大男人愣是从床上爬了起来。不管怎么说，她知道，她的朋友在工作日早上出来跟她碰头，是做出了一点牺牲的。他整晚都要上班，白天睡觉。她看见他站在说好碰头的地方，柬埔寨大使馆门前的街角，冲着她挥手。过了一会儿，他的手不挥了——因为她仍旧离得好远——接着，稍后，他又挥起来。她也朝她挥手。终于走到他跟前时，他们的手握到了一起，这个动作让他们自己也吓了一跳。“我的羽毛球打得可好了，”他们俩经过柬埔寨大使馆时，安德鲁说，“我会打到你哭着求饶！下一回，我们别游泳了，找个地方打羽毛球吧。”下一回，我们应该去巴黎。下一回，我们应该到月亮上去。他是个梦想家。话说回来，比起有些事情来，当个梦想家还算好的。

0－20

“所以你本身是一位客人，而这是你的客人?”柜台后面的姑娘问道。

“我是一位客人，而这是另一位客人。”法图答道。

“哦……按规矩不能这样的吧?”

“求你了，”法图说，“我们过来走了很长的路。”

“我很感动，”女孩说，“可我真的不应该让你进去，实话实说。”

“求你了。”法图又说了一次。她也想不出还有什么别的说辞。

女孩拿出一支钢笔，在法图的入场券上做了个记号。

“只此一次。我这么干请你千万别说出去。下不为例！我得算你两次进馆。”

于是，只此一次下不为例，安德鲁和法图一起来到更衣室，各自从男士和女士两扇门进去。在女更衣室，法图用闪电般的速度换好衣服。可是她一出来就看到安德鲁已经上了一把躺椅，双眼盯着女更衣室，等她出来。

“伙计，这才是生活!”他一边说，一边把胳膊枕到脑后。

“你下水吗?”法图问道，她努力装作在不经意间把双手挡在了腹股沟前面。

“现在还不下，伙计，我只想把这些看看真切，全都看个遍。你下去吧。我一会儿就来。”

法图沿着梯子爬下去，开始游泳。动作并不优雅，却游得特别快，连贯持久，坚实有力。时不时地，她会偏过头来看看安德鲁是不是还躺在椅子上兀自微笑。二十圈之后，她游到他的躺椅附近，用手肘撑住瓷砖。

“你不下水吗？水可暖和啦。就像洗澡一样。”

“当然，当然，”他说，“我会试试的。”

他坐起来，肚皮上的肉折叠起来，法图不禁怀疑，刚才他一直待在躺椅上，就是为了不让她看见他的肚子到底有多大，肉又是怎么晃晃悠悠的。他朝梯子这边走过来；法图向他伸出一只手，被他推开。他自己下来，站在浅水区，像王子那样往肩膀上浇水，然后弓起身子钻进水里。

“真暖和！好舒服。这才是生活，伙计！你在前面游——我跟着你。”

法图一蹬腿，激起水花一大片，她听见隔壁泳道上有人在抱怨。她一口气游到池壁，转身找安德鲁。他的游法——反正看起来是这样——先是深深潜入水中，像只河马那样悬在那里，然后，等到非得吸口气时他才举起胳膊连拍带打地冒出来，接着又潜下去，悬在水中。这样游，很短的距离就要耗掉很多体力，等他捱到池壁时，已是上气不接下气。他的眼睛——他没戴泳镜——红得厉害。

“没事的，”法图说，想再拉住他的手。“要是你肯学，我就教你怎么游。”可他放开她的手，直擦眼睛。

“这池子里该死的氯气太多啦。”

“你想走?”

安德鲁转身看着法图。他的眼睛在流泪。法图觉得他看起来就像是个小男孩，在竭力掩饰他刚才哭过。不过，紧接着，他在水下拉住她的手。

“不走。我只想在这里放松放松。”

“好吧。”法图说。

“你去游。你不错。你游。”

“好吧。”法图说，再度出发，可她发觉自己每游一圈，心思就比前一圈更涣散，节奏也越发紊乱。她可不习惯游泳的时候被人盯着看。十圈之后，她突然在泳道正中站起来，走完剩下的路，直到池壁。

“你想用爵士按摩浴缸吗?”她问他，朝浴缸指了指。

热乎乎的浴缸里坐着一个女人，身穿一套湿透的田径服，头上裹着头巾。有个男人坐在她身边，可能是她丈夫，他一边盯着法图看，一边对女人说了点什么。他身上的毛可真是又浓又密，简直就像是跟她穿得一样多。他们俩双双从水中站起身，走开了。男人穿着最小号的速比涛泳裤，就是法图原先最怕安德鲁穿的那种裤子，还好他没穿成那样。安德鲁的短裤非常合适，长度及膝，红得纯粹，很衬他的肤色。

“不用，”安德鲁说，“只要跟你一起待着，看着全世界从这里经过，就很好了。”

0－21

那天晚上，法图给解雇了。不是因为会员入场券的事——德拉瓦尔家从来没发觉法图用他们的会籍在泳池里游了多少英里。说实话，法图也很难理解她到底为什么会给解雇，就连德拉瓦尔太太自己似乎也没法解释清楚。

“你不明白，我们不需要保姆，”她说，人站在法图的房间门口——那房间压根站不下两个人，除非其中有一个躺在床上。“孩子们都长大了。我们需要一个人来操持家务，能把家里打扫干净。这些天，你对孩子要比对打扫房间更上心。”法图压根就不喜欢那几个孩子，一点儿都不喜欢，可是德拉瓦尔太太还在往下说。“这样一来，你对我们就没什么用了。”

法图一言不发。她在想自己连一个正经行李箱都没有，只能把东西装进塑料袋，从德拉瓦尔先生家的房子搬出去。

“所以说，你得尽快找个别的住处啦。”德拉瓦尔太太说。

“我先生的表亲礼拜五要来，就住这个房间——就这个礼拜五。”

法图琢磨了一会儿，然后说，“我可以打一个电话吗?”

德拉瓦尔太太在打量一块从门框上剥落的木片。可她还是点了点头。

“我想把我的护照要回来，请你给我。”

“什么?”

“请把护照还给我。”

末了，德拉瓦尔太太看着法图，直视她双眼，可她的脸扭作一团，就好像法图刚刚走到她面前扇过她耳光似的。谁都看得出来，魔鬼已经爬到了可怜的德拉瓦尔太太身上。他点燃了她的一腔怒火。

“看在老天分上，小妞，我没有你的护照！我要你的护照做什么用？弄不好在什么厨房的哪个抽屉里。替你找东西难道也归我管吗?”

她走了，撇下法图一个人。她把自己的东西装进平时带去泳池的那些给她打掩护的购物袋里。就在她忙活的时候，有人从门缝里把她的护照塞进来。一小时之后，她拎起袋子下楼，直接走到客厅的电话机旁。法伊祖尔路过，举起手来想跟她击掌。法图没理她，径自拨通安德鲁的电话。从她朋友说话的声音里，她能听出他是被她吵醒的，可他一丁点儿都没生气。他听法图把非说不可的话说出来，然后，不等她提醒，他似乎就已经明白，现在她说话不方便。她刚说完，他就飞快地问了几个实在的问题，然后把他的打算清晰而认真地解释了一遍。

“不会有什么问题的。他们办公室需要清洁工——我会去帮你问的。在这段时间里，你就到我这里来。我们轮换着睡。你可以相信我。我是尊重你的，法图。”

可她没有公交卡；卡在厨房里，被一枚印着佛罗里达风光的磁贴压在冰箱表面。她宁愿死也不想再到那里去。这也没问题：晚上六点，他可以在布朗德斯伯里站接她。法图看看面前的那台落地大摆钟：她还有四个小时要打发。

“六点。”她又念叨了一遍。她放下电话，从仿路易十六时期的螺形托脚小桌的抽屉里拿出所有剩下的入场券，离开了那栋宅子。

“今天有点沉重嘛。”柜台后面的女孩一边说，一边冲着法图手里的塑料袋点点头。法图拿出一张入场券给她盖章，脸上没有笑。一个半小时之后，法图大步走过柜台，还是那个女孩对她说：“下回见。”法图心情依然沉重，依然不愿意为了那女孩以前帮过她的忙而流露出一丁点感激来。感激是另一种奴役。你最好还是能“自有安排”。

走出门，四周灰蒙蒙冷飕飕，法图觉得自己被水洗得通体洁净，心情也为之明亮，无论是天气还是新环境都不会让它黯淡无光。她的四肢仍然疲软无力，头发也仍然没干；这样站在外面，弄不好要感冒。才四点半。她把塑料袋往人行道上一搁，自己坐在边上，她的位置紧挨着公交车站，对面就是柬埔寨大使馆。公交车一辆辆地来又一辆辆地走，老是为她放慢车速，看她没有上车的意思，只好再猛然加速，飞奔向前。那天午后，我们有很多人从她身边走过，要不就是坐在公交车上、透过汽车挡风玻璃或者站在阳台上看见她。顺理成章地，我们都在纳闷，正午时分，这姑娘一直坐在湿漉漉的人行道上，她到底在干什么。我们替她担心。在威尔斯登，我们总是会想到最可怕的情形。我们看着她看着羽毛球的样子。击球，扣杀。击球，扣杀。好像一方只能想象用一个暴戾的结局结束战斗，而另一方只会怀着希望把球打回去。

译后记

扎迪·史密斯似乎是那种天生就能从大城市的喧嚣芜杂中听出交响合唱的作家。从《白牙》到《签名收藏家》、《美》，再到 2012 年在大西洋两岸均引起热烈反响的《西北》，史密斯洞察并描摹现代城市不同阶层、族裔生存状态的技术愈见纯熟。有时候，史密斯的这种能力甚至在一些规模更小的作品中表现得更为集中和充分，比如这部起先发表在 2013 年的《纽约客》杂志，后来以单行本形式出版的小说《使馆楼》。

英国报章把《使馆楼》比喻成一台智能手机，尺寸玲珑却内藏乾坤。这话大抵是说这个短篇的单位信息量远远超过了平均水准，却又组织得自然妥帖、井井有条。读完这篇小说，你的记忆里会清晰地留下伦敦威尔斯登地区的一条街，街上的住户“多半是富庶的阿拉伯人”。非洲裔姑娘法图是一个巴基斯坦中产家庭的住家保姆，没有工资，也几乎没有可以自由支配的时间，除了每周一上午偷偷使用这家人的会员入场券，从街的一头走到另一头，到一个高档健身中心游泳——这点小小的冒险，这段短短的旅程，是法图艰辛生活中的亮点。

小说照例要起波澜。这次是这户人家的孩子出了一点意外，恰巧被法图化解。然而救命之恩反倒打破了主仆关系原有的平衡，史密斯寥寥数笔就把这种吊诡的转变刻画得入木三分。法图面临被无端解雇的命运，她有点迷茫，却并未失去希望。至此，此前种种关乎心灵的铺陈——法图莫名被柬埔寨大使馆建筑吸引的瞬间，使馆楼围墙上飞来飞去的羽毛球（“击球，扣杀”……），她与来自尼日利亚的教友安德鲁的约会与讨论，那些关于信仰与现实的只字片语，仿佛都生出藤蔓来，彼此勾连成一张网。正如这条短短的街道，承载着族裔、阶层之间的碰撞，顿时也成了整个伦敦，乃至整个世界的缩影。

小说的视角跟着法图走，但叙述却仿佛是通过一个更抽象、更超然的声音实现的——有时候这个声音是“我”，更多的时候，则是“我们”。对此，英国媒体同样给出了饶有趣味的比喻：“就像古希腊合唱团”。具体地说，这样做不仅能在法图的个体经历中注入普遍意义，而且在叙述中平添一层反讽色彩，比如：“几年前，柬埔寨大使馆第一次出现在我们这一带时，有人说，‘呃，假如我们是诗人，看到大使馆突然出现在这里，没准能写出一首颂诗之类的玩意。’（因为大使馆通常都在市中心。我们这是头一回在郊区看到使馆楼。）可我们终究也不是什么诗兴盎然的人。我们是威尔斯登人。我们的趣味总是乏善可陈。”

无论从哪个角度看，《使馆楼》都是两千年之后具有示范意义的短篇小说。它在一个标准短篇的容量中嵌入了中篇小说的结构，又以娴熟的技巧和广阔的视野，使读者得到类似于长篇小说的阅读体验。透过法图的遭遇，我们既对现代大都市的痼疾感同身受，又会在这位新移民越来越清晰而坚定的自我认知中看到些许微茫的希望——而后者，在一部直击现实、不回避任何阴暗面的小说中，通常是很难处理得令人信服的。史密斯不仅做了，而且做得很好。

或许正因为如此，史密斯本人对《使馆楼》十分偏爱，不愿归入短篇小说集，而是坚持要将它作为一部独立的作品出版。中译本采用双语对照方式，并配上熟谙伦敦街景的马岱姝女士绘制的插图，力图呈现这种短篇文字的独特韵律和字里行间强烈的画面感。一个你从任何旅游指南上都看不见的伦敦，一个更痛切、更辛酸也更斑斓的伦敦，就藏在这区区几万字的褶皱里。

黄昱宁

2016 年 5 月

The Embassy of Cambodia

0 – 1

Who would expect the Embassy of Cambodia? Nobody. Nobody could have expected it, or be expecting it. It's a surprise, to us all. The Embassy of Cambodia!

Next door to the embassy is a health centre. On the other side, a row of private residences, most of them belonging to wealthy Arabs (or so we, the people of Willesden, contend). They tend to have Corinthian pillars on either side of their front doors, and—it's widely believed—swimming pools out the back. The embassy, by contrast, is not very grand. It is only a four-or five-bedroom north London suburban villa, built at some point in the 1930s, surrounded by a red-brick wall, about eight feet high. And back and forth, cresting this wall horizontally, flies a shuttlecock. They are playing badminton in the Embassy of Cambodia. Pock, smash. Pock, smash.

The only real sign that the embassy is an embassy at all is the little brass plaque on the door (which reads: 'THE EMBASSY OF CAMBODIA') and the national flag of Cambodia (we assume that's what it is—what else could it be?) flying from the red-tiled roof. Some say, 'Oh, but it has a high wall around it, and this is what signifies that it is not a private residence, like the other houses on the street, but rather an embassy.' The people who say so are foolish. Many of the private houses have high walls, quite as high as the Embassy of Cambodia—but they are not embassies.

0 -2

On 6 August, Fatou walked past the embassy for the first time, on her way to a swimming pool. It is a large pool, although not quite Olympic size. To swim a mile you must complete eighty-two lengths, which, in its very tedium, often feels as much a mental exercise as a physical one. The water is kept unusually warm, to please the majority of people who patronize the health centre, the kind who come not so much to swim as to lounge poolside or rest their bodies in the sauna. Fatou has swum here five or six times now, and she is often the youngest person in the pool by several decades. Generally, the clientele are white, or else South Asian or from the Middle East, but now and then Fatou finds herself in the water with fellow Africans. When she spots these big men, paddling frantically like babies, struggling simply to stay afloat, she prides herself on her own abilities, having taught herself to swim, several years earlier, at the Carib Beach

Resort, in Accra. Not in the hotel pool—no employees were allowed in the pool. No, she learned by struggling through the rough grey sea, on the other side of the resort walls. Rising and sinking, rising and sinking, on the dirty foam. No tourist ever stepped on to the beach (it was covered with trash), much less into the cold and treacherous sea. Nor did any of the other chambermaids. Only some reckless teenage boys, late at night, and Fatou, early in the morning. There is almost no way to compare swimming at Carib Beach and swimming in the health centre, warm as it is, tranquil as a bath. And, as Fatou passes the Embassy of Cambodia, on her way to the pool, over the high wall she sees a shuttlecock, passed back and forth between two unseen players. The shuttlecock floats in a wide arc softly rightwards, and is smashed back, and this happens again and again, the first player always somehow able to retrieve the smash and transform it, once more, into a gentle, floating arc. High above, the sun tries to force its way through a cloud ceiling, grey and filled with water. Pock, smash. Pock, smash.

0 – 3

When the Embassy of Cambodia first appeared in our midst, a few years ago, some of us said, 'Well, if we were poets perhaps we could have written some sort of an ode about this surprising appearance of the embassy.' (For embassies are usually to be found in the centre of the city. This was the first one we had seen in the suburbs.) But we are not really a poetic people. We are from Willesden. Our minds tend towards the prosaic. I doubt there is a man or woman among us, for example, who—upon passing the Embassy of Cambodia for the first time—did not immediately think: 'genocide'.

0 - 4

Pock, smash. Pock, smash. This summer we watched the Olympics, becoming well attuned to grunting, and to the many other human sounds associated with effort and the triumph of the will. But the players in the garden of the Embassy of Cambodia are silent. (We can't say for sure that it is a garden—we have a limited view over the wall. It may well be a paved area, reserved for badminton.) The only sign that a game of badminton is under way at all is the motion of the shuttlecock itself, alternately being lobbed and smashed, lobbed and smashed, and always at the hour that Fatou passes on her way to the health centre to swim (just after ten in the morning on Mondays). It should be explained that it is Fatou's employers—and not Fatou—who are the true members of this health club; they have no idea she uses their guest passes in this way. (Mr and Mrs Derawal and their three children—aged seventeen, fifteen and ten—live on the same street as the embassy, but the road is almost a mile long, with the embassy at one end and the Derawals at the other.) Fatou's deception is possible only because on Mondays Mr Derawal drives to Eltham to visit his mini-market there, and Mrs Derawal works the counter in the family's second mini-mart, in Kensal Rise. In the slim drawer of a faux-Louis XVI console, in the entrance hall of the Derawals' primary residence, one can find a stockpile of guest passes. Nobody besides Fatou seems to remember that they are there.

Since 6 August (the first occasion on which

she noticed the badminton), Fatou has made a point of pausing by the bus stop opposite the embassy for five or ten minutes before she goes in to swim, idle minutes she can hardly afford (Mrs Derawal returns to the house at lunchtime) and yet seems unable to forgo. Such is the strangely compelling aura of the embassy. Usually, Fatou gains nothing from this waiting and observing, but on a few occasions she has seen people arrive at the embassy and watched as they are buzzed through the gate. Young white people carrying rucksacks. Often they are scruffy, and wearing sandals, despite the cool weather. None of the visitors so far have been visibly Cambodian. These young people are likely looking for visas. They are buzzed in and then pass through the gate, although Fatou would really have to stand on top of the bus stop to get a view of whoever it is that lets them in. What she can say with certainty is that these occasional arrivals have absolutely no effect on the badminton, which continues in its steady pattern, first gentle, then fast, first soft and high, then hard and low.

0 – 5

On 20 August, long after the Olympians had returned to their respective countries, Fatou noticed that a basketball hoop had appeared in the far corner of the garden, its net of synthetic white rope rising high enough to be seen over the wall. But no basketball was ever played—at least not when Fatou was passing. The following week it had been moved closer to Fatou's side of the wall. (It must be a mobile hoop, on casters.) Fatou waited a week, two weeks, but still no basketball game replaced the badminton, which carried on as before.

0 - 6

When I say that we were surprised by the appearance of the Embassy of Cambodia, I don't mean to suggest that the embassy is in any way unique in its peculiarity. In fact, this long, wide street is notable for a number of curious buildings, in the context of which the Embassy of Cambodia does not seem especially strange.

There is a mansion called GARYLAND, with something else in Arabic engraved below GARYLAND, and both the English and the Arabic text are inlaid in pink-and-green marble pillars that bookend a gigantic fence, far higher than the embassy's, better suited to a fortress. Dramatic golden gates open automatically to let vehicles in and out. At any one time, GARYLAND has five to seven cars parked in its driveway.

There is a house with a huge pink elephant on the doorstep, apparently made of mosaic tiles.

There is a Catholic nunnery with a single red Ford Focus parked in front. There is a Sikh institute. There is a faux-Tudor house with a pool that Mickey Rooney rented for a season, while he was performing in the West End fifteen summers ago. That house sits opposite a dingy retirement home, where one sometimes sees distressed souls, barely covered by their dressing gowns, standing on their tiny balconies, staring into the tops of the chestnut trees.

So we are hardly strangers to curious buildings, here in Willesden and Brondesbury. And yet still we find the Embassy of Cambodia a little surprising. It is not the right sort of surprise, somehow.

0 – 7

In a discarded *Metro* found on the floor of the Derawal kitchen, Fatou read with interest a story about a Sudanese 'slave' living in a rich man's house in London. It was not the first time that Fatou had wondered if she herself was a slave, but this story, brief as it was, confirmed in her own mind that she was not. After all, it was her father, and not a kidnapper, who had taken her from Ivory Coast to Ghana, and when they reached Accra they had both found employment in the same hotel. Two years later, when she was eighteen, it was her father again who had organized her difficult passage to Libya and then on to Italy—a not insignificant financial sacrifice on his part. Also, Fatou could read English—and speak a little Italian—and this girl in the paper could not read or speak anything except the language of her tribe. And nobody beat Fatou, although Mrs Derawal had twice slapped her in the face, and the two older children spoke to her with no respect at all and thanked her for nothing. (Sometimes she heard her name used as a term of abuse between them. 'You're as black as Fatou.' Or 'You're as stupid as Fatou.') On the other hand, just like the girl in the newspaper, she had not seen her passport with her own eyes since she arrived at the Derawals', and she had been told from the start that her wages were to be retained by the Derawals to pay for the food and water and heat she would require during her stay, as well as to cover the rent for the room she slept in. In the final analysis, however, Fatou was not confined to the house. She had an Oyster Card, given to her by the Derawals, and was trusted to do the food shopping and other outside tasks, for which she was given cash and told to return with change and receipts for everything. If she did not go out in the evenings that was only because she had no money with which to go out, and anyway knew very few people in London. Whereas the girl in the paper was not allowed to leave her employers' premises, not ever—she was a prisoner.

On Sunday mornings, for example, Fatou regularly left the house, to meet her church friend Andrew Okonkwo at the 98 bus stop and go with him to worship at the Sacred Heart of Jesus, just off the Kilburn High Road. Afterwards Andrew always took her to a Tunisian café, where they had coffee and cake, which Andrew, who worked as a night guard in the City, always paid for. And on Mondays Fatou swam. In very warm water, and thankful for the semi-darkness in which the health club, for some reason, kept its clientele, as if the place were a nightclub, or a midnight Mass. The darkness helped disguise the fact that her swimming costume was in fact a sturdy black bra and a pair of plain black cotton knickers. No, on balance she did not think she was a slave.

0 – 8

The woman exiting the Embassy of Cambodia did not look especially like a New Person or an Old Person—neither clearly of the city nor the country—and of course it is a long time since this division meant anything in Cambodia. Nor did these terms mean anything to Fatou, who was curious only to catch her first sighting of a possible Cambodian anywhere near the Embassy of Cambodia. She was particularly interested in the woman's clothes, which were precise and utilitarian—a grey shirt tucked tightly into a pair of tan slacks, a blue mackintosh, a droopy rain hat—just as if she were a man, or no different from a man. Her straight black hair was cut short. She had in her hands many bags from Sainsbury's, and this Fatou found a little mysterious: where was she taking all that shopping? It also surprised her that the woman from the Embassy of Cambodia should shop in the same Willesden branch of Sainsbury's where Fatou shopped for the Derawals. She had an idea that Oriental people had their own, secret establishments and shopped there. (She believed the Jews did, too.) She both admired and slightly resented this self-reliance, but had no doubt that it was the secret to holding great power, as a people. For example, when the Chinese had come to Fatou's village to take over the mine, an abiding local mystery had been: what did they eat and where did they eat it? They certainly did not buy food in the market, or from the Lebanese traders along the main road. They made their own arrangements. (Whether back home or here, the key to surviving as a people, in Fatou's opinion, was to make your own arrangements.)

But, looking again at the bags the Cambodian woman carried, Fatou wondered whether they weren't in fact very old bags—hadn't their design changed? The more she looked at them the more convinced she became that they contained not food but clothes or something else again, the outline of each bag being a little too rounded and smooth. Maybe she was simply taking out the rubbish. Fatou stood at the bus stop and watched until the Cambodian woman reached the corner, crossed and turned left towards the high road.

Meanwhile, back at the embassy the badminton continued to be played, though with a little more effort now because of a wayward wind. At one point it seemed to Fatou that the next lob would blow southwards, sending the shuttlecock over the wall to land lightly in her own hands. Instead the other player, with his vicious reliability (Fatou had long ago decided that both players were men), caught the shuttlecock as it began to drift and sent it back to his opponent—another deathly, downward smash.

0 – 9

No doubt there are those who will be critical of the narrow, essentially local scope of Fatou's interest in the Cambodian woman from the Embassy of Cambodia, but we, the people of Willesden, have some sympathy with her attitude. The fact is if we followed the history of every little country in this world—in its dramatic as well as its quiet times—we would have no space left in which to live our own lives or to apply ourselves to our necessary tasks, never mind indulge in occasional pleasures, like swimming. Surely there is something to be said for drawing a circle around our attention and remaining within that circle. But how large should this circle be?

0 – 10

It was the Sunday after Fatou saw the Cambodian that she decided to put a version of this question to Andrew, as they sat in the Tunisian café eating two large fingers of dough stuffed with cream and custard and topped with a strip of chocolate icing. Specifically, she began a conversation with Andrew about the Holocaust, as

Andrew was the only person she had found in London with whom she could have these deep conversations, partly because he was patient and sympathetic to her, but also because he was an educated person, presently studying for a part-time business degree at the College of North West London. With his student card he had been given free, twenty-four-hour access to the Internet.

'But more people died in Rwanda,' Fatou argued. 'And nobody speaks about that! Nobody!'

'Yes, I think that's true,' Andrew conceded, and put the first of four sugars in his coffee. 'I have to check. But, yes, millions and millions. They hide the true numbers, but you can see them online. There's always a lot of hiding; it's the same all over. It's like this bureaucratic Nigerian government—they are the greatest at numerology, hiding figures, changing them to suit their purposes. I have a name for it: I call it "demonology". Not "numerology" — "demonology".'

'Yes, but what I am saying is like this,' Fatou pressed, wary of the conversation's drifting back, as it usually did, to the financial corruption of the Nigerian government. 'Are we born to suffer? Sometimes I think we were born to suffer more than all the rest.'

Andrew pushed his professorial glasses up his nose. 'But, Fatou, you're forgetting the most important thing. Who cried most for Jesus? His mother. Who cries most for you? Your father. It's very logical, when you break it down. The Jews cry for the Jews. The Russians cry for the Russians. We cry for Africa, because we are Africans, and, even then, I'm sorry, Fatou' — Andrew's chubby face creased up in a smile— 'if Nigeria plays Ivory Coast and we beat you into the ground, I'm laughing, man! I can't lie. I'm celebrating. Stomp! Stomp!'

He did a little dance with his upper body, and Fatou tried, not for the first time, to imagine what he might be like as a husband, but could see only herself as the wife, and Andrew as a teenage son of hers, bright and helpful, to be sure, but a son all the same—though in reality he was three years older than she. Surely it was wrong to find his baby fat and struggling moustache so off-putting. Here was a good man! She knew that he cared for her, was clean and had given his life to Christ. Still, some part of her rebelled against him, some unholy part.

'Hush your mouth,' she said, trying to sound more playful than disgusted, and was relieved when he stopped jiggling and laid both his hands on the table, his face suddenly quite solemn.

'Believe me, that's a natural law, Fatou, pure and simple. Only God cries for us all, because we are *all* his children. It's very, very logical. You just have to think about it for a moment.'

Fatou sighed, and spooned some coffee foam into her mouth. 'But I still think we have more pain. I've seen it myself. Chinese people have never been slaves. They are always protected from the worst.'

Andrew took off his glasses and rubbed them on the end of his shirt. Fatou could tell that he was preparing to lay knowledge upon her.

'Fatou, think about it for a moment, please: what about Hiroshima?'

It was a name Fatou had heard before, but sometimes Andrew's superior knowledge made her nervous. She would find herself struggling to remember even the things she had believed she already knew.

'The big wave ...' she began, uncertainly—it was the wrong answer. He laughed mightily and shook his head at her.

'No, man! Big bomb. Biggest bomb in the world, made by the USA, of course. They killed five million people in *one second*. Can you imagine that? You think just because your eyes are like this' —he tugged the skin at both temples— 'you're always protected? Think again. This bomb, even if it didn't blow you up, a week later it melted the skin off your bones.'

Fatou realized she had heard this story before, or some version of it. But she felt the same vague impatience with it as she did with all accounts of suffering in the distant past. For what could be done about the suffering of the distant past?

'OK,' she said. 'Maybe all people have their hard times, in the past of history, but I still say—'

'Here is a counterpoint,' Andrew said, reaching out and gripping her shoulder. 'Let me ask you, Fatou, seriously, think about this. I'm sorry to interrupt you, but I have thought a lot about this and I want to pass it on to you, because I know you care about things seriously, not like these people—' He waved a hand at the assortment of cake eaters at other tables. 'You're not like the other girls I know, just thinking about the club and their hair. You're a person who thinks. I told you before, anything you want to know about, ask me—I'll look it up, I'll do the research. I have access. Then I'll bring it to you.'

'You're a very good friend to me, Andrew, I know that.'

'Listen, we are friends to each other. In this world you need friends. But, Fatou, listen to my question. It's a counterpoint to what you have been saying. Tell me, why would God choose us especially for suffering when we, above all others, praise his name? Africa is the fastest-growing Christian continent! Just think about it for a minute! It doesn't even make sense!'

'But it's not him,' Fatou said quietly, looking over Andrew's shoulder to the rain beating on the window. 'It's the Devil.'

0 – 11

Andrew and Fatou sat in the Tunisian coffee shop, waiting for it to stop raining, but it did not stop raining and at three p. m. Fatou said she would just have to get wet. She shared Andrew's umbrella as far as the Overground, letting him pull her into his clammy, high-smelling body as they walked. At Brondesbury station Andrew had to get the train, and so they said goodbye. Several times he tried to press his umbrella on her, but Fatou knew the walk from Acton Central to Andrew's bedsit was long and she refused to let him suffer on her account.

'Big woman. Won't let anybody protect you.'

'Rain doesn't scare me.'

Fatou took from her pocket a swimming cap she had found on the floor of the health club changing room. She wound her plaits into a bun and pulled the cap over her head.

'That's a very original idea,' Andrew said, laughing. 'You should market that! Make your first million!'

'Peace be with you,' Fatou said, and kissed him chastely on the cheek.

Andrew did the same, lingering a little longer with his kiss than was necessary.

0 – 12

By the time Fatou reached the Derawals' only her hair was dry, but before going to get changed she rushed to the kitchen to take the lamb out of the freezer, though it was pointless—there were not enough hours before dinner—and then upstairs to collect the dirty clothes from the matching wicker baskets in four different bedrooms. There was no one in the master bedroom, or in Faizul's or Julie's. Downstairs a television was blaring. Entering Asma's room, hearing nothing, assuming it empty, Fatou headed straight for the laundry basket in the corner. As she opened the lid she felt a hand hit her hard on the back; she turned around.

There was the youngest, Asma, in front of her, her mouth open like a trout fish. Before Fatou could understand, Asma punched the huge pile of clothes out of her hands. Fatou stooped to retrieve them. While she was kneeling on the floor, another strike came, a kick to her arm.

She left the clothes where they were and got up, frightened by her own anger. But when she looked at Asma now she saw the girl gesturing frantically at her own throat, then putting her hands together in prayer and then back to her throat once more. Her eyes were bulging. She veered suddenly to the right; she threw herself over the back of a chair. When she turned back to Fatou her face was grey and Fatou understood finally and ran to her, grabbed her round her waist and pulled upwards as she had been taught in the hotel. A marble—with an iridescent ribbon of blue at its centre, like a wave—flew from the child's mouth and landed wetly in the carpet's plush.

Asma wept and drew in frantic gulps of air. Fatou gave her a hug, and worried when the clothes would get done. Together they went down to the den, where the rest of the family was watching *Britain's Got Talent* on a flat-screen TV attached to the wall. Everybody stood at the sight of Asma's wild weeping. Mr Derawal paused the Sky box. Fatou explained about the marble.

'How many times I tell you not to put things in your mouth?' Mr Derawal asked, and Mrs

Derawal said something in their language—Fatou heard the name of their God—and pulled Asma on to the sofa and stroked her daughter's silky black hair.

'I couldn't breathe, man! I couldn't call nobody,' Asma cried. 'I was gonna die!'

'What you putting marbles in your mouth for anyway, you idiot?' Faizul said, and unpaused the Sky box. 'What kind of chief puts a marble in her mouth? Idiot. Bet you was bricking it.'

'Oi, she saved your life,' said Julie, the eldest child, whom Fatou generally liked the least.

'Fatou saved your life. That's deep.'

'I woulda just done this,' Faizul said, and performed an especially dramatic Heimlich to his own skinny body. 'And if that didn't work I woulda just start pounding myself karate style, bam bam bam bam bam—'

'Faizul!' Mr Derawal shouted, and then turned stiffly to Fatou, and spoke not to her, exactly, but to a point somewhere between her elbow and the sunburst mirror behind her head. 'Thank you, Fatou. It's lucky you were there.'

Fatou nodded and went to leave, but at the doorway to the den Mrs Derawal asked her if the lamb had defrosted and Fatou had to confess that she had only just taken it out. Mrs Derawal said something sharply in her language. Fatou waited for something further, but Mr Derawal only smiled awkwardly at her, and nodded as a sign that she could go now. Fatou went upstairs to collect the clothes.

0 – 13

'To keep you is no benefit. To destroy you is no loss' was one of the mottoes of the Khmer Rouge. It referred to the New People, those city dwellers who could not be made to give up city life and work on a farm. By returning everybody back to the land, the regime hoped to create a society of Old People—that is to say, of agrarian peasants. When a New Person was relocated from the city to the country, it was vital not to show weakness in the fields. Vulnerability was punishable by death.

In Willesden, we are almost all New People, though some of us, like Fatou, were, until quite recently, Old People, working the land in our various countries of origin. Of the Old and New People of Willesden I speak; I have been chosen to speak for them, though they did not choose me and must wonder what gives me the right. I could say, 'Because I was born at the crossroads of Willesden, Kilburn and Queen's Park!' But the reply would be swift and damning: 'Oh, don't be foolish, many people were born right there; it doesn't mean anything at all. We are not one people and no one can speak for us. It's all a lot of nonsense. We see you standing on the balcony, overlooking the Embassy of Cambodia, in your dressing gown, staring into the chestnut trees, looking gormless. The real reason you speak in this way is because you can't think of anything better to do.'

0 – 14

On Monday, Fatou went swimming. She paused to watch the badminton. She thought that the arm that delivered the smashes must make a movement similar to the one she made in the pool, with her clumsy yet effective front crawl. She entered the health centre and gave a guest pass to the girl behind the desk. In the dimly lit changing room, she put on her sturdy black underwear. As she swam, she thought of Carib Beach. Her father serving snapper to the guests on the deck, his bow tie always a little askew, the ugly tourists, the whole scene there. Of course, it was not surprising in the least to see old white men from Germany with beautiful local girls on their laps, but she would never forget the two old white women from England—red women, really, thanks to the sun—each of them as big as two women put together, with Kweku and Osai lying by their sides, the boys hooking their scrawny black bird-arms round the women's massive red shoulders, and dancing with them in the hotel 'ballroom', answering to the names Michael and David, and disappearing into the women's cabins at night. She had known the boys' real girlfriends; they were chambermaids like Fatou. Sometimes they cleaned the rooms where Kweku and Osai spent the night with the English women. And the girls themselves had 'boyfriends' among the guests. It was not a holy place, that hotel. And the pool was shaped like a kidney bean: nobody could really swim in it, or showed any sign of wanting to. Mostly, they stood in it and drank cocktails.

Sometimes they even had their burgers delivered to the pool. Fatou hated to watch her father crouching to hand a burger to a man waist-high in water.

The only good thing that happened in Carib Beach was this: once a month, on a Sunday, the congregation of a local church poured out of a coach at the front gates, lined up fully dressed in the courtyard and then walked into the pool for a mass baptism. The tourists were never warned, and Fatou never understood why the congregants were allowed to do it. But she loved to watch their white shirts bloat and spread across the surface of the water, and to hear the weeping and singing. At the time—though she was not then a member of that church, or of any church except the one in her heart—she had felt that this baptism was for her, too, and that it kept her safe, and that this was somehow the reason she did not become one of the 'girls' at the Carib Beach Resort. In almost two years—between her father's efforts and the grace of an unseen and unacknowledged God—she did her work, and swam Sunday mornings at the crack of dawn, and got along all right. But the Devil was waiting.

She had only a month left in Accra when she entered a bedroom to clean it one morning and heard the door shut softly behind her before she could put a hand to it. He came, this time, in Russian form. Afterwards, he cried and begged her not to tell anyone: his wife had gone to see the Cape Coast Castle and they were leaving the following morning. Fatou listened to his blubbering and realized that he thought the hotel would punish him for his action, or that the police would be called. That was when she knew that the Devil was stupid as well as evil. She spat in his face and left. Thinking about the Devil now made her swimming fast and angry, and for a while she easily lapped the young white man in the lane next to hers, the faster lane.

0 – 15

'Don't give the Devil your anger, it is his food,' Andrew said to her, when they first met, a year ago. He handed her a leaflet as she sat eating a sandwich on a bench in Kilburn Park. 'Don't make it so easy for him.' Without being invited, he took the seat next to hers and began going through the text of his leaflet. It was printed to look like a newspaper, and he started with the headline: 'WHY IS THERE PAIN?' She liked him. They began a theological conversation. It continued in the Tunisian café, and every Sunday for several months. A lot of the things he said she had heard before from other people, and they did not succeed in changing her attitude. In the end, it was one thing that he said to her that really made the difference. It was after she'd told him this story:

'One day, at the hotel, I heard a commotion on the beach. It was early morning. I went out and I saw nine children washed up dead on the beach. Ten or eleven years old, boys and girls. They had gone into the water, but they didn't know how to swim. Some people were crying, maybe two people. Everyone else just shook their heads and carried on walking to where they were going. After a long time, the police came. The bodies were taken away. People said, "Well, they are with God now." Everybody carried on like before. I went back to work. The next year I was in Rome. I saw a boy who was about fifteen years old knocked down on his bike. He was dead. People were screaming and crying in the street. Everybody crying. They were not his family. They were only strangers. The next day, it was in the paper.'

And Andrew replied, 'A tap runs fast the first time you switch it on.'

0 – 16

Twenty more laps. Fatou tried to think of the last time she had cried. It was in Rome, but it wasn't for the boy on the bike. She was cleaning toilets in a Catholic girls' school. She did not know Jesus then, so it made no difference what kind of school it was—she only knew she was cleaning toilets. At midday, she had a fifteen-minute break. She would go to the little walled garden across the road to smoke a cigarette. One day, she was sitting on a bench near a fountain and spotted something odd in the bushes. A tin of green paint. A gold spray can. A Statue of Liberty costume. An identity card with the name Rajib Devanga. One shoe. An empty wallet. A plastic tub with a slit cut in the top meant for coins and euro notes—empty. A little stain of what looked like blood on this tub. Until that point, she had been envious of the Bengali boys on Via Nazionale. She felt that she, too, could paint herself green and stand still for an hour.

But when she tried to find out more the Bengalis would not talk to her. It was a closed shop, for brown men only. Her place was in the toilet stalls. She thought those men had it easy. Then she saw that little sad pile of belongings in the bush and cried; for herself or for Rajib, she wasn't sure.

Now she turned on to her back in the water for the final two laps, relaxed her arms and kicked her feet out like a frog. Water made her think of more water. 'When you're baptized in our church, all sin is wiped, you start again': Andrew's promise. She had never told Andrew of the sin precisely, but she knew that he knew she was not a virgin. The day she finally became a Catholic, 6 February 2011, Andrew had taken her, hair still wet, to the Tunisian café and asked her how it felt.

She was joyful! She said, 'I feel like a new person!'

But happiness like that is hard to hold on to. Back at work the next day, picking Julie's dirty underwear up off the floor inches from the wicker basket, she had to keep reminding herself of her new relationship with Jesus and how it changed everything. Didn't it change everything? The following Sunday she expressed some of her doubt, cautiously, to Andrew.

'But did you think you'd never feel sad again? Never angry or tired or just pissed off—sorry about my language. Come on, Fatou! Wise up, man!'

Was it wrong to hope to be happy?

0 – 17

Lost to these watery thoughts, Fatou got home a little later than usual and was through the door only minutes before Mrs Derawal.

'How is Asma?' Fatou asked. She had heard the girl cry out in the night.

'My goodness, it was just a little marble,' Mrs Derawal said, and Fatou realized that it was not in her imagination: since Sunday night, neither of the adult Derawals had been able to look her in the eye. 'What a fuss everybody is making. I have a list for you—it's on the table.'

0 – 18

Fatou watched Andrew pick his way through the tables in the Tunisian café, holding a tray with a pair of mochas on it and some croissants. He hit the elbow of one man with his backside and then trailed the belt of his long, silly leather coat through the lunch of another, apologizing as he went. You could not say he was an elegant man. But he was generous, he was thoughtful. She stood up to push a teetering croissant back on to its plate. They sat down at the same time, and smiled at each other.

'A while ago you asked me about Cambodia,' Andrew said. 'Well, it's a very interesting case.' He tapped the frame of his glasses. 'If you even wore a pair of these? They would kill you. Glasses meant you thought too much. They had very primitive ideas. They were enemies of logic and progress. They wanted everybody to go back to the country and live like simple people.'

'But sometimes it's true that things are simpler in the country.'

'In some ways. I don't really know. I've never lived in the country.'

I don't really know. It was good to hear him say that! It was a good sign. She smiled cheekily at him. 'People are less sinful in the country,' she said, but he did not seem to see she was flirting with him, and began upon another lecture.

'That's true. But you can't force people to live in the country. That's what I call a Big Man Policy. I invented this phrase for my dissertation. We know all about Big Man Policies in Nigeria. They come from the top and they crush you. There's always somebody who wants to be the Big Man, and take everything for themselves, and tell everybody how to think and what to do. When, actually, it's he who is weak. But if the Big Men see that *you* see that *they* are weak they have no choice but to destroy you. That is the real tragedy.'

Fatou sighed. 'I never met a man who didn't want to tell everybody how to think and what to do,' she said.

Andrew laughed. 'Fatou, you include me? Are you a feminist now, too?'

Fatou brought her mug up to her lips and

looked penetratingly at Andrew. There were good and bad kinds of weakness in men, and she had come to the conclusion that the key was to know which kind you were dealing with.

'Andrew,' she said, putting her hand on his, 'would you like to come swimming with me?'

0 – 19

Because Fatou believed that the Derawals' neighbours had been instructed to spy on her, she would not let Andrew come to the house to pick her up on Monday, instead leaving as she always did, just before ten, carrying misleading Sainsbury's bags and walking towards the health centre. She spotted him from a long way off—the road was so straight and he had arrived early. He stood shivering in the drizzle. She felt sorry, but also a little prideful: it was the prospect of seeing her body that had raised this big man from his bed. Still, it was a sacrifice, she knew, for her friend to come out to meet her on a weekday morning. He worked all night long and kept the daytime for sleeping. She watched him waving at her from their agreed meeting spot, just on the corner, in front of the Embassy of Cambodia. After a while, he stopped waving—because she was still so far away—and then, a little later, he began waving again. She waved back, and when she finally reached him they surprised each other by holding hands. 'I'm an excellent badminton player,' Andrew said, as they passed the Embassy of Cambodia. 'I would make you weep for mercy! Next time, instead of swimming we should play badminton somewhere.' Next time, we should go to Paris. Next time, we should go to the moon. He was a dreamer. But there are worse things, Fatou thought, than being a dreamer.

0 – 20

'So you're a guest and this is your guest?' the girl behind the desk asked.

'I am a guest and this is another guest,' Fatou replied.

'Yeah . . . that's not really how it works?'

'Please,' Fatou said. 'We've come from a long way.'

'I appreciate that,' the girl said. 'But I really shouldn't let you in, to be honest.'

'Please,' Fatou said again. She could think of no other argument.

The girl took out a pen and made a mark on Fatou's guest pass.

'This one time. Don't tell no one I did this, please. One time only! I'll need to cross off two separate visits.'

For one time only, then, Andrew and Fatou approached the changing rooms together and parted at the doors that led to the men's and the women's. In her changing room, Fatou got ready with lightning speed. Yet somehow he was already there on a lounger when she came out, eyes trained on the women's changing-room door, waiting for her to emerge.

'Man, this is the life!' he said, putting his arms behind his head.

'Are you getting in?' Fatou asked, and tried to place her hands, casually, in front of her groin.

'Not yet, man, I'm just taking it all in, taking it all in. You go in. I'll come in a moment.'

Fatou climbed down the steps and began to swim. Not elegant, not especially fast, but consistent and determined. Every now and then she would angle her head to try to see if Andrew was still on his chair, smiling to himself. After twenty laps, she swam to where he lay and put her elbows on the tiles.

'You're not coming in? It's so warm. Like a bath.'

'Sure, sure,' he said. 'I'll try it.'

As he sat up his stomach folded in on itself, and Fatou wondered whether he had spent all that time on the lounger to avoid her seeing its precise bulk and wobble. He came towards the stairs; Fatou held out a hand to him, but he pushed it away. He made his way down and stood in the shallow end, splashing water over his shoulders like a prince fanning himself, and then crouching down into it.

'It is warm! Very nice. This is the life, man! You go, swim—I'll follow you.'

Fatou kicked off, creating so much splash she heard someone in the adjacent lane complain. At the wall, she turned and looked for Andrew. His method, such as it was, involved dipping deep under the water and hanging there like a hippo, then batting his arms till he crested for air, and then diving down again and hanging. It was a lot of energy to expend on a short distance, and by the time he reached the wall he was panting like a maniac. His eyes—he had no goggles—were painfully red.

'It's OK,' Fatou said, trying to take his hand again. 'If you let me, I'll show you how.' But he shrugged her off and rubbed at his eyes.

'There's too much bloody chlorine in this pool.'

'You want to leave?'

Andrew turned back to look at Fatou. His eyes were streaming. He looked, to Fatou, like a little boy trying to disguise the fact he had been crying. But then he held her hand, under the water.

'No. I'm just going to take it easy right here.'

'OK,' Fatou said.

'You swim. You're good. You swim.'

'OK,' Fatou said, and set off, and she found that each lap was more distracted and rhythmless than the last. She was not used to being watched while she swam. Ten laps later, she suddenly stood up halfway down the lane and walked the rest of the distance to the wall.

'You want to go in the Jacuzzi?' she asked him, pointing to it.

In the hot tub sat a woman dressed in a soaking tracksuit, her head covered with a headscarf. A man next to the woman, perhaps her husband, stared at Fatou and said something to the woman. He was so hairy he was almost as covered as she was. Together they rose up out of the water and left. He was wearing the tiniest of Speedos, the kind Fatou had feared Andrew might wear, and was grateful he had not. Andrew's shorts were perfectly nice, knee-length, red and solid, and looked good against his skin.

'No,' Andrew said. 'It's great just to be here with you, watching the world go by.'

0－21

That same evening, Fatou was fired. Not for the guest passes—the Derawals never found out how many miles Fatou had travelled on their membership. In fact, it was hard for Fatou to understand exactly why she was being fired, as Mrs Derawal herself did not seem able to explain it very precisely.

'What you don't understand is that we have no need for a nanny,' she said, standing in the doorway of Fatou's room—there was not really enough space in there for two people to stand without one of them being practically on the bed. 'The children are grown. We need a housekeeper, one who cleans properly. These days, you care more about the children than the cleaning,' Mrs Derawal added, though Fatou had never cared for the children, not even slightly. 'And that is of no use to us.'

Fatou said nothing. She was thinking that she did not have a proper suitcase and would have to take her things from Mrs Derawal's house in plastic bags.

'And so you will want to find somewhere else to live as soon as possible,' Mrs Derawal said. 'My husband's cousin is coming to stay in this room on Friday—this Friday.'

Fatou thought about that for a moment. Then she said, 'Can I please use the phone for one call?'

Mrs Derawal inspected a piece of wood that had flaked from the doorframe. But she nodded.

'And I would like to have my passport, please.'

'Excuse me?'

'My passport, please.'

At last Mrs Derawal looked at Fatou, right into her eyes, but her face was twisted, as if Fatou had just reached over and slapped her. Anyone could see the Devil had climbed inside poor Mrs Derawal. He was lighting her up with a pure fury.

'For goodness' sake, girl, I don't have your passport! What would I want with your passport? It's probably in a drawer in the kitchen somewhere. Is that my job now, too, to look for your things?'

•

Fatou was left alone. She packed her things into the decoy shopping bags she usually took to the swimming pool. While she was doing this, someone pushed her passport under her door. An hour later she carried her bags downstairs and went directly to the phone in the hall. Faizul walked by and lifted his hand for a high-five. Fatou ignored him and dialled Andrew's number. From her friend's voice she knew that she had woken him, but he was not even the slightest bit angry. He listened to all she had to say and seemed to understand, too, without her having to say so, that at this moment she could not speak freely. After she had said her part, he asked a few quick technical questions and then explained clearly and carefully what was to happen.

'It will all be OK. They need cleaners in my offices—I will ask for you. In the meantime, you come here. We'll sleep in shifts. You can trust me. I respect you, Fatou.'

But she did not have her Oyster Card; it was in the kitchen, on the fridge under a magnet of Florida, and she would rather die than go in there. Fine: he could meet her at six p. m. at Brondesbury Overground station. Fatou looked at the grandfather clock in front of her: she had four hours to kill.

'Six o'clock,' she repeated. She put the phone down, took the rest of the guest passes from the drawer of the faux-Louis XVI console and left the house.

'Weighed down a bit today,' the girl at the desk of the health club said, nodding at Fatou's collection of plastic bags. Fatou held out a guest pass for a stamp and did not smile. 'See you next time,' this same girl said, an hour and a half later, as Fatou strode past, still weighed down and still unwilling to be grateful for past favours. Gratitude was just another kind of servitude. Better to make your own arrangements.

Walking out into the cold grey, Fatou felt a sense of brightness, of being washed clean, that neither the weather nor her new circumstances could dim. Still, her limbs were weary and her hair was wet; she would probably catch a cold, waiting out here. It was only four thirty. She put her bags on the pavement and sat down next to them, just by the bus stop opposite the Embassy of Cambodia. Buses came and went, slowing down for her and then jerking forward when they realized that she had no interest in getting up and on. Many of us walked past her that afternoon, or spotted her as we rode the bus, or through the windscreens of our cars, or from our balconies. Naturally, we wondered what this girl was doing, sitting on the damp pavement in the middle of the day. We worried for her. We tend to assume the worst, here in Willesden. We watched her watching the shuttlecock. Pock, smash. Pock, smash. As if one player could imagine only a violent conclusion and the other only a hopeful return.

扎迪·史密斯谈种族、女性与文学创作

张　芸

自二十五岁那年携《白牙》一举震惊文坛后，如今的扎迪·史密斯（Zadie Smith）俨然成为英国青年一代作家的代表，以其讽刺幽默的文风、节奏鲜明的叙事、丰富的语言表现力捕捉着隐藏在当代社会庸常生活背后繁杂的冲突与隔阂，并被推举为“种族、年轻、女性”的代言人。然而，除了出众的写作能力，她还是一个敢言善论的批评家、一个流行文化的关注者、一个针砭时事的通讯作者……简言之，你绝不能简单地用她的小说去定义她。

您的小说《美》和《西北》新近出了中译本，根据这两本书的创作时间，我们先聊一聊《美》。它的故事主要发生在大波士顿地区，您恰好曾在哈佛大学担任过访问学者，请问，这本小说与您本人的经历有怎样的关系？

史密斯：我开始在拉德克利夫（Radcliffe）研究院，那以前是一间女校，后来到哈佛待了一年，我在那儿度过了一个非常寒冷的冬天。要说里面最有自传色彩的元素，应该是雪，到处是厚厚的积雪，这些雪自然被我写进了小说。但更具体来讲，小说里的故事素材更多来自另一个剑桥，英国剑桥。我对学术生活的许多感想源自我在英国剑桥的经历，而不是美国。

原来如此。您是英国人，也在美国的几所大学教授小说写作，从您的角度看，美国的大学生活和英国的有什么不同？

史密斯： 我觉得现在来讲，两者变得越来越近似。但在我上大学的年代，在英国，大学是免费的，在那种条件下，学生和教授之间的关系与现在不同。教授在我心目中是相当崇高、高贵的，他们的薪水不丰，但却有着卓越的学识和才华，因此，和他们的关系，有点类似和牧师或医生的关系。而在美国，大学和钱密切挂钩，学费很高，所以师生关系更倾向于服务性质，我为这些学生打工，因为他们付钱来上学，让我有薪水。

小说《美》刻画了自由派和保守派之间的观念冲突。有调查显示，近一二十年来，大部分美国大学的教授支持和认同自由派，在英国也是一样的情形吗?

史密斯：就我自己而言，我喜欢称自己是人道主义者。我应该属于自由派，但我不愿给自己贴上这个标签，我知道眼下，在许多大学的保守派中间，存在一种害怕自由派大行其道的恐慌，例如在纽约大学，这种情况特别显著。从一个角度讲，人道主义的部分观点与自由派是一致的，两者都强调开明和争论的相对性，所以人道主义从本质上讲是自由主义，这一点很难反驳。但我在教学过程中，尽量对各种不同的观点，无论是政治还是宗教方面的信念，保持开放的态度，注意到学生可能持有的不同理念，避免让我的教学变成说教。

小说里有一位主人公是受邀到美国担任访问学者的英国教授，这种局外人的身份，是否在一定程度上使他更容易在美国大学里发出保守派的声音？

史密斯：说到蒙蒂，我觉得他算不上是一个真正意识形态上的保守派，他的成长环境决定了他更像是个异议分子，他只是非常看不惯自由派，他的反应其实可能发生在任何人身上。他天生具有反对派的个性，他讨厌仅因为他的种族背景他就必须成为什么样的人的预设，这是一种更深层的叛逆，他想要做的是颠覆人们对他的期许。所以，我不觉得他有多么保守，在我看来，他更像是一个喜欢质疑、反抗的挑衅式人物。

在小说里，还有一些人物，总在努力寻找归属感，比如霍华德的儿子利瓦伊，他喜欢和贫民区的黑人男孩混在一起，觉得自己同他们更亲近，而抵触他生来所属的那个精英世界。您怎么看待这样一种身份认同的焦虑?

史密斯：我笔下的人物通常和我自己是不一样的。就我本人来讲，“我是谁”、“我在别人眼中是什么人”，这些问题虽然重要，但我觉得有比它们更重要的问题：“我应该做什么”、“我的责任和义务是什么”。的确，作为人，人们对你有一个印象和定位，如果在别人眼里找不到对你的定义，那是成问题的。但当你在他人眼中有了明确的身份和定位后，我认为，这并不能解决人生中实际遇到的难题，在某种意义上，这只是一个开端。所以，我虽然相信我们需要寻找身份认同，但另一方面，我觉得这没有那么的重要。

您自己有过这方面的身份困扰吗？

史密斯：没有。我不是那种经常思考“我是谁”或“我不是谁”的人，虽然我塑造的人物时常受困于其中。我可以说我自己是英国人、黑人、女人，这些是客观事实，但这些事实对我起不了太大帮助，不能教会我怎么在这个世上生存和立足。我觉得“如何在这个世界上生存和立足”才是更基本的、超越“你是谁”的存在问题。

这部小说的名字叫作“美”，似乎含有一层反讽意味，因为小说里的故事有时并不那么美好。尤其到

结尾的高潮，局面几乎变得一发不可收拾，活像一出闹剧，令人发噱。能否请您谈谈这种喜剧元素在您作品中的分量和作用?

史密斯：我觉得喜剧是一种美。我明白，从严格意义上说，喜剧缺少升华的特质，但我认为，作为生活的一部分，喜剧是具有美感的。因此，对我而言，很难在作品中不掺入喜剧元素。换句话说，喜剧是我感受这个世界的一种方式和角度，我曾颇为努力地试图遏制我作品中的喜剧色彩，但后来放弃了，因为我发现这是我创作中与生俱来的元素。我的一个弟弟是表演单人喜剧的，所以我想这大概是我们家的遗传吧。

去年，我有机会翻译了奇玛曼达·阿迪契的小说《美国佬》，这本书给了我全新的视野，让我认识黑

人。书中的主人公有一句话令我印象深刻，她说，她到了美国才意识到自己是黑人。您出生在伦敦，您的母亲是牙买加人，父亲是英国人，能否请您聊一聊，作为一个黑人和白人的混血儿在英国成长的经历?

史密斯：我的经历和奇玛曼达不同。我始终知道我是黑人，那是我周围的世界给我的定义。当我后来去西非的时候，我能完全体会她笔下主人公那番话的含义，感受到自己不是众人中的一员。我觉得这种感到自己与周遭人不一样的经验，发生在每个走入陌生环境里的人身上，我猜移居海外的中国人也有类似的感受，自己变成别人眼中的他者。不过，这提供了一个有趣的认识自己的视角，把自己放在彻底异类的位置上，从历史角度讲，各方面，不同的背景、属性，追溯到不同的血统乃至人种，在我看来，这是一个有意思的立场。

当一个别人眼中的他者，这不是一件容易的事吧？

史密斯：我向来认为，人活在世上是不容易的。各人有各人的难处。但这些难处通常源于感觉自己被人误贴标签，感觉别人不了解自己或了解得不够，换言之，问题总是由外而来，加诸你身上，而不是你本身所有的。就我自己来说，我想我总是怀着一种好奇，想知道自己可能是个怎样的人。

现在您住在英美两地，请问，在美国和英国，黑人的处境有所不同吗？

史密斯：很多人问我这个问题。的确不一样。首先，历史根源不同，黑人最早以奴隶身份踏上美国这片土地，这与从殖民地移民宗主国的方式截然不同。具体来讲，黑人在美国和英国的境遇千差万别，各有优劣，但有一点我更欣赏美国：人们公开明确地讨论种族问题，我觉得这比遮遮掩掩强。

继《美》之后，您创作了小说《西北》。这部小说的叙事风格与《美》迥然不同，以碎片拼贴、非线性时间的方式组织故事。一般来说，您是怎么确定一部小说的叙事手法和形式的？

史密斯：我觉得这是一个作者很难给出理性回答的问题。好比绘画，一个画家从风格上可以分为不同的时期，如蓝色时期、红色时期、抽象时期、具象时期，但若问那个画家，为什么这幅画是蓝色，那幅是红色，他恐怕难以给出理性的解答。一方面，我们可以说，主题决定形式；另一方面，就我个人而言，我不喜欢重复同样的写法，我会厌倦。

所以是有故事在先？

史密斯：那样说也不对。通常在写一本小说时，我并没有计划好的故事大纲。通常我有的是一个细微、模糊的想法，然后我会尝试寻找一定的笔调、口吻去表述。这个过程可能会很久、很艰难，但一旦找到准确的调子后，接下来就水到渠成了。就像画家，在画第一笔前，要在调色板上找到准确的色调，那可能需要漫长的时间。

在《西北》里，主人公利娅是她工作团队里唯一的白人，这令我想起《美》里面的琪琪，在和她丈夫

的朋友、同事聚会时，察觉到自己是众人中唯一的黑人，因而感到不自在。这种隔阂，似乎是您小说要表现的一个重要主题?

史密斯：绝对是。我认为，当人们在一个环境里感到不自在或无法完全融入时，那提供了一个可发挥的创造性空间。当你和一个环境完全融合、在里面如鱼得水、没有丝毫距离感时，你不大会对很多东西提出质疑，一种怠惰会在头脑里油然而生。只有当你置身于一个与你不相容的环境时，比如白人在非洲，当他们第一次发现或体验到自己是少数族裔时，那常常会引发相当有趣的思考，是他们以前没有想过的。对我而言，这是一种有益的心态，让人对事物、对现实更投入。

所以对小说而言，这也是一种很好的故事素材。

史密斯：是的。我自己有过很多这类隔阂的经验，那为创作小说提供了丰富的源泉，去想象或突然间意识到一切都不是注定或必然的，人生的种种取决于当下的情况，完全存在另外的可能。对我来说，这是创作小说的原动力，即探索事情的多种可能性。

小说中的另外一位主人公娜塔莉/凯莎，竭尽全力挣脱她原本的出身，可她的成功，在她的家人眼中却被视为某种背叛。您觉得，这是想要出人头地者经常会面临的两难境地吗?

史密斯：据我的观察，以纽约为例，在很多新的华人移民家庭中，有一个突出的现象，子女一辈融入美国的生活，说一口流利的英语，并在事业上取得不小的成就，但他们的父母依旧保持着他们刚来时的状态，他们可能不讲英语，对他们而言，不仅与自己的祖国分离，也和他们的子女分离，这是一般土生土长的美国人很难想象的经验。在你接受教育的同时，却和你的家人离得越来越远，甚至变得像陌生人，这种境况，想来是匪夷所思的。从父母的角度讲，这是他们做出的巨大牺牲，他们为了孩子的前程而献出了自己与孩子间的纽带。这不是一种容易相处的关系，我觉得这里面藏着几分动人而哀伤的味道。

的确，这样的故事也出现在别的小说里，比如伊丽莎白·斯特劳特的新书《我叫露西·巴顿》（My Name is Lucy Barton），讲一个家境贫寒的姑娘长大后成了知名作家，但与家人的关系疏离紧张。

史密斯：我知道，我等不及要读这本书。诚然，几乎每个工人阶级背景出身的作家身上，都有这样一个真实的狄更斯式的故事。当你积极投入创作时，你与你的家人从根本上分道扬镳。以我自己为例，我的父亲从未读过我的小说，这是一种颇耐人寻味的感受，不一定就是残酷无情，只是你不可能、没有办法建立那座联结的桥梁。

在小说里，利娅和娜塔莉相信，大家都认为她们应当生儿育女，娜塔莉按人们的期许照做了，而利娅始终犹疑不决，这一分歧给她们的友谊蒙上了阴影。您怎么看待这样一种普遍的认为女性应当为人母的观点?

史密斯：在这点上，我真正感兴趣的是，当一件从生物学和社会学角度来讲不可避免的事，转变成另外一种性质的问题，一个选择性的问题时，是怎样的情形，这是我想探究的。千禧一代的女性在生儿育女的问题上变得可以有选择，这理当被视为一种解放和自由，我同意。可另一方面，生活里有很多东西，选择并不是最重要的。很多时候，当你有权利选择一样东西时，你可能不会接受它，但那不表示这样东西没有价值或意义。在我这一代女性的身上，引起我兴趣的一件事是，她们会互相倾诉："我想不好到底要不要小孩，因为我还没决定，所以暂时不能要小孩。"生儿育女仿佛成了一件主动去争取和渴望的事，这实际是一个脱离历史语境的想法。当母亲的人不一定内心真的想要小孩，但孩子就是来了。这不是一个你想不想要的问题。当你把这个问题变成一种选择时，那给人感觉其实是下策。我觉得很有趣的是那些调查研究表明，有孩子的人比没孩子的人过得凄惨，这其实是在挑战我们对人生的认知，人生的目标是什么，是追求时刻的快乐、永恒的快乐，还是别的，是某些注定要发生的东西。所以我关心的不是从道德伦理上去讨论“要不要小孩”的问题，而是当一种生物本能被重新包装、以选择题的形式呈现时，那会出现什么情况。我不相信人活在世上可以挣脱一切束缚，人生不是将万事自由化，人生中存在某些限制，什么样的限制是不可通融的呢?

小说中的娜塔莉对自己的人生有十分清楚的规划，什么时候做什么，包括什么时候生小孩。这是不

是女人的某种特质，对时间格外敏感，由于女性本身特有的生物钟的关系？

史密斯：我以前是这么认为的，但与此同时，女人亦有一种强大的自欺欺人的本领。比如我的朋友中，有比较晚生小孩的女性，你若问她们，你可意识到，等你女儿十六岁时，你都五十八岁了，她们会震惊不已，不敢相信，可这不过是一道简单的数学题呀。在对时间的认识上，女人有时会忘记这些最基本的事实。一种故意的自欺欺人。我自己也曾有过这样的震惊，虽然我明知那是事实，但从别人口中讲出来，还是觉得讶异。所以我猜，我想必有某种强大的本领，能够每天逃避承认时间的存在——这个我人生最基本的事实。

诚如书名《西北》所示，这部小说的故事发生在伦敦西北区，这一区也出现在您其他的小说和短篇里。可否请您谈一谈，这个特定的地域在您小说创作中扮演的重要角色?

史密斯：这片地区一直是我创作中必不可少的元素。但我发现，不只是我，所有和我一起长大的人，以及生活在那一带的居民，对那片地区都怀有特殊的感情。说不定，伦敦每片地区都是这样。我的两个弟弟，一个做电视节目，一个是说唱歌手，他们的作品里也经常提到伦敦西北区。我的朋友去参加校友聚会，甚至可能试想回到以前住的街道定居。我觉得这是挺普遍的现象，在伦敦，每片街坊具有某种自成一格的特色。有时，倘若我去伦敦南区，会遇到那种兴高采烈、对当地几条街道特别着迷的人，虽然那些街道其实毫无意思，但对他们而言却意义重大。这是城市的特别之处吧。可能不只伦敦，每个城市，如纽约也是如此，每片街坊总有其忠实的居民。

现在，您一部分时间住在伦敦，一部分时间住在纽约，能否讲讲您对纽约的感受？

史密斯：我很喜欢在纽约格林威治村的生活，这个地方对我有不凡的意义，那是我以前没有料到的。说来有些讽刺，大家都知道，格林威治村的风光时期已成过去，这里不再有鲍勃·迪伦，不再有激进的运动，街上少了年轻人的身影，但尽管如此，这里还是活跃着某些东西，那令人惊奇。还是有年轻的艺术家、歌手、喜剧演员、街头艺人出现在这里。撇开游客和金融新贵不论，华盛顿广场公园，天热时，即使到深夜，仍是一处能让人感到兴奋和刺激的场所。所以，虽然这已不再是六十年代或四十年代的格林威治村——那个被传为神话的地方——但我爱这里。在住了七年以后，我开始意识到，现在的格林威治村同样有趣，是 2016 年版的格林威治村。这种爱，与你对故乡的热爱，是不同的。

您年少时好像曾有过想当舞蹈演员或歌手的志向，那么，您是什么时候发现自己真正想从事的是写作？

史密斯：我并没有真的想成为舞蹈演员或歌手。我喜欢私下里唱歌跳舞，但我讨厌表演，只要一登台，舞台必然被我搞砸。我非常怯场，不喜欢在人前表演，那太叫人紧张和难受。我向来更专注的是读书和看电影。我的弟弟是演员，通过他，我能清晰地想象出演员是一份什么样的工作。做演员太无力，那不是我想要的，对我有吸引力的往往是我能掌控的东西。虽然歌唱和舞蹈是我的爱好，但我很小的时候就明白，那是需要遵从指示的活动，而我不愿意那样做。

从个人爱好的角度讲，私下里的唱歌跳舞，对您的写作有所助益吗?

史密斯：有，这三者有相通的地方。我觉得我们家的每个成员都有很强的节奏感，虽然我们从事的工作不同，但都可归结于节奏和模仿。或者说，我们都有灵敏的耳朵。一双灵敏的耳朵，可以有助于你唱歌、演奏乐器、讲台词、说笑话、写作。在我看来，这是一种才华，一种散布在不同领域的相同的才华。

可否请您展开说一说写作中的节奏感？

史密斯：就写作来讲，有一双灵敏的耳朵，意味着知道准确的调子、准确的进度，甚至是落在纸上的准确的形象。就像跳舞时，我一边听着鼓点，一边知道身体该放在哪个位置，写作也类似。

我想起以前采访科尔姆·托宾，他也格外强调节奏是他创作的关键。

史密斯：对，托宾是一位非常注重节奏和韵律的小说家，他也是个大乐迷。很多作家，甚至文学评论家，像著名的詹姆斯·伍德，在音乐方面也颇有造诣。我觉得，当作家，可以有许多软肋，比如缺乏对人物内心的洞察力、不幽默风趣、不懂情节为何物，这些不足，不是一个作家的致命伤。但假如你没有一双会听的耳朵，你就无法入门。在我看来，那是写作唯一不可或缺的要素。

这很有意思，因为事实上，无论写作还是阅读，都是无声的活动。

史密斯：的确，但每当我翻开一本书时，我能立刻听到里面的声音。对我而言，情节合不合理，是其次的、表面的东西，我用听去判断一个人会不会写作。这包含了音乐性的问题。

您有两个小孩，既要写作，又要当母亲，兼顾两者是不是很不容易?

史密斯：我觉得和所有的职业女性一样，我的情况没有比她们更难。最大的问题是时间，如何分配和管理时间。虽然有时写作可能需要投入更多时间，但另一方面，它对时间的要求更灵活。在纽约，许多上班的母亲无法接送小孩上学或参加活动，但我可以，因为我能自由调整我的工作时间，我可以一早写作，或晚上写作，全由我自己决定。这种灵活性，对我而言是好事。

您也给《纽约书评》等杂志撰写评论和散文，非虚构写作与虚构写作会互相影响吗？

史密斯：非虚构写作要求把事情讲得清楚明白，让人满意。虚构性的作品则有更多矛盾和不确定，更多想法藏而不露。另外，对我来说，撰写评论或散文是一件可以在短时间内完成的工作，那可以增添我的自信心，表示我在工作上有进展。创作小说的困难是，那需要花上好几年时间，有时会在一个地方卡住很久，这很令人受挫。相比之下，写评论比较容易让我有成就感。

图书在版编目(CIP)数据

使馆楼:汉、英/(英)扎迪·史密斯(Zadie Smith)著;黄昱宁译.
—上海:上海译文出版社,2017.1
书名原文:The Embassy of Cambodia
ISBN 978-7-5327-7280-3

Ⅰ.①使… Ⅱ.①扎…②黄… Ⅲ.①短篇小说—英国—现代—汉、英 Ⅳ.①I561.45

中国版本图书馆 CIP 数据核字(2016)第 119496 号

图字:09-2015-045 号

使馆楼(中英双语珍藏本)

[英]扎迪·史密斯 著 黄昱宁 译
责任编辑/杨懿晶 装帧设计/胡 枫

上海世纪出版股份有限公司
译文出版社出版
网址:www.yiwen.com.cn
上海世纪出版股份有限公司发行中心发行
200001 上海福建中路 193 号 www.ewen.co
苏州市越洋印刷有限公司印刷

开本 787×1092 1/32 印张 7.25 插页 5 字数 40,000
2017 年 1 月第 1 版 2017 年 1 月第 1 次印刷
印数:0,001-5,000 册

ISBN 978-7-5327-7280-3/I·4431
定价:38.00 元